Wrong Number to *Right* Person

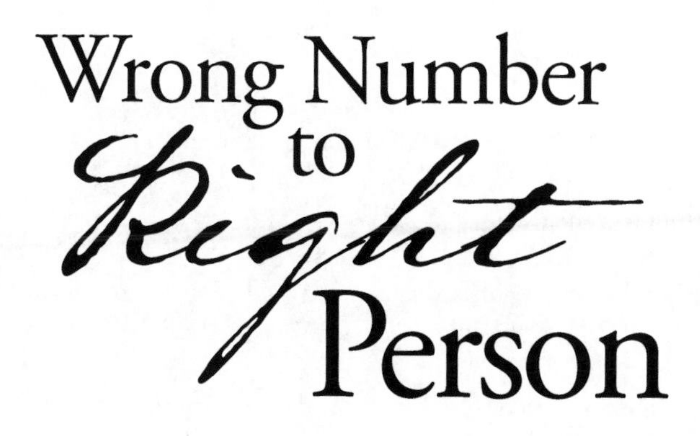

NISHIGANDHA OMANWAR

nishihere@gmail.com

ISBN:	Softcover	978-1-4828-1695-2
	Ebook	978-1-4828-1694-5

To order additional copies of this book, contact
Partridge India
000 800 10062 62
www.partridgepublishing.com/india
orders.india@partridgepublishing.com

CONTENTS

Chap 1 Day at Adlabs 1
Chap 2 The Mysterious call 12
Chap 3 The Surprise 18
Chap 4 The Answered Prayer 25
Chap 5 The Growing Friendship–I 33
Chap 6 The Growing Friendship–II 42
Chap 7 He Loves Me? 56
Chap 8 Love Blossoms 67
Chap 9 The Ugly Truth 82
Chap 10 Visit to TVM 95
Chap 11 Racing with Time 109
Chap 12 The Restless call 121
Chap 13 Letter from Madhav 131
Chap 14 The Past Returns 138

A few comments I received for my writing. I chose to print voice of comman man, common in all terms just like you and me so that you can relate to them.

☘ I don't know what to write I can just say I loved each and every character in story which shows wonderful you represented each character.

The language usage in story and interest creation in ending of each part is very good.

In one word simply superb . . .

—Prafulla

☘ I really liked story very much.Eagerly looking forward to the sequel and Very happy to hear that you are converting them into story books.

Wish you all the best for your future endeavors! Keep writing . . . & keep smiling

—Prachi

☘ I really loved your work. I am a bad reader; I hate reading whether it's a story, novel or study books. The characters created by you are so real that I can feel their pain as if it's happening to me. I just wanted to appreciate you for your superb work. You have a great talent, do not stop writing.

—Ruchika

☘ What to say. I just loved the way u cage feeling into words.

The more I read d more I fall in love wid dis story.

I not only imagine but feel it.

—Shruti

☘ It was really good to read your story. Although I am not a love story buff, I still enjoyed it.

You really have a good sense of penning down thoughts and emotions which is a rare gift and even harder an chievement if gained by practice. Keep writing.

—Mandar

☘ Nicely written story . . . kept me engrossed till the end . . .

Nicely mentioned the love and friendship . . . nice ending too . . .

Wish that u get to publish a book soon . . .

All the Best!!!

—Akshat

☘ U r really a gr8 writer . . . Kudos to u for this . . .

Ur writings make ppl desperate to wait for the next chapters . . . keep it up . . .

It ws really a nice article to read . . .

—Ankit

Brilliant work . . . absonalutely brilliant . . . .

Best of luck for your bright future . . . hope i see another Chetan Bhagat in near future. Best of luck dear.

—Rahul

Story is well written and excellent narration of each and every feelings, it's very tough to keep in words what we feel, I very rarely read but after I started reading your story, I was very eagerly waiting for next part everyday . . .

—Shilpa

It was awosome . . . Plz keep on writing. the end was expected and u described it very nicely . . . especially the letter written by Maddy was described very nicely, we can really imagine it and felt as if we are watching a movie . . . could not wait at all till today, so read it yest itself on ur blog . . . you really have a talent to be an author great job . . . keep it up

—Ana

Awesome:) Wonderful narration Nishi. i felt like i was seeing the characters infront on every part. Keep Writing!!

—Sara

This story was outstanding . . . i have read dhdm first then i read this story and i loved both of them . . . keep it up

—Vini

Wow, excellent one . . . loved it . . . really loved the way you expressed . . . How lively you explained each and everything, felt like it was happening infront of my eyes . . . All the best . . . [:)]

—Harshu

Hi Nishi . . . I liked this story a lot . . . ur way of representing and thinking is damn good . . . keep writing more blogs as i have become a big fan of ur writing [:)]

—Vivek

I feel so connected to this story Nishi . . .

Beutiful!!! Unable to resist for the next one indeed [:)]

—RSwan

It is so interesting and then I found your blog where I found all other parts . . . I just read these all parts in 3 hours . . . .

WOW!!! what a story it is . . .

Heartly thanks

—Darshit

☘ I have followed all the parts of the story.

It was a nice reading with a good climax and well articulated. I will surely read your blog to read your future writings.

And last but not the least . . . All the best for your future endeavors outside of Infy.

☘ The story was awesome . . . Nishi . . . I just read all parts . . . Your imagination is extraordinary . . . I liked the way you narrated the story . . . Awaiting your next story . . .

—Hiru

☘ U story is rocking 1 . . . i didn't saw any faults in your writing . . . bcz I was totally lost in ur story . . . Newys, gr8t writing and keep going . . .

All d best.

—Raman

☘ Story Was awesome Nishi . . . i read all d parts off the story it was tooogood. Now m eagerly waiting for ur next story . . . :-)

—Sneha

☘ U must be surprised to see my mail . . . but what should i do . . . i m such a big fan of ur writings. ur bolgs are mind blowin . . . superbly awesome. the sole purpose of this mail is to appreciate you for all your writings . . . n wish you keep continue writing . . .

—Khushboo

☘ I am a big fan of all ur blogs . . . Not less than watching a romantic movie . . . Liked ur story . . . really good . . . When I read thru, I could imagine the story being happening in real . . . You have such good story writing skills whoever read once can't stop themselves to read the next part . . . the way you have penned down this story its really commendable . . .

—Anju

☘ I have no words to say Nishi. You know, in between my work I was reading these parts and it made me to read completely and then continue with work.

Great work. Keep it up. :)

—Deepa

☘ Very nice story and close to my heart [:)] . . . i really loved it . . .

—Shala

☘ Awesome yar . . . keep writing . . .

—Radhika

♣ I read quite a lot. At least from my college days.

I try so many titles. But only a few interest me. And definitely your works are also very attractive.

The way the story is taken. It brings back our own memories. Thanks a lot for that . . .

I really want your stories to be published . . .

All the best with that.

—Subramanian

♣ Excellent dear . . . really not getting words to express . . . awesome writing!!!!

—Archana

♣ Well narrated. Appreciate your thoughts to words.

—Nitin

Dedicated to my loving husband . . .

"I love the way you make me smile . . .

. . . even when you are not around."

ACKNOWLEDGMENTS

This book would have not been into prints without the encouragement from my colleagues in Infosys and Wipro; Infosys planted a dream seed in my heart and Wipro watered it, and today my dream is breathing and living, it is a reality. I want to thank you all; it's because of you that I could realize this. You who read my write ups and encouraged me, filled my eyes with a dream, I would have never known that my writings interest people. Without your word of praise which persuaded me to dream, to see, my name on a books cover page. If I start naming I may fall short of space but you know your name is in this list.

A dream never realizes in dreams! We need to work hard for it; I would like to thank my loving husband for being with me in every step of bringing this dream of mine to life and for standing by my side in tough time. It took long to achieve this but I now know the wait was worth.

A special mention for designers of the book cover,
Front Cover By: Deepak Vimal.
Back Cover By: Abhilash Meher.

I hope you love reading this story
as much as I loved writing it!

PROLOGUE

Have you ever got a call from a wrong number? I know the answer is yes, but have your missed something very important because of this call, a call from an unknown person and you miss the most awaited moment of your life?

How many times in a day do you get a call from a wrong number, may be once in a day or once in a week but what if you get call from a wrong number several times? Will you be irritated? How many times can you tell someone that it is a wrong number that they have dialed? You talk to the unknown person politely! You don't know why? Should we call it destiny—may be. You are destined to talk to the person, what if the other person sounds interesting, you engage in talks with him and slowly you become phone friend, and what if you take this relation ahead and fall in love with him, falling in love with someone you haven't met? Haven't seen? Do you feel the excitement of knowing more about such person, excitement to meet this new love?

This story is of Tanvi who attends a call from Wrong number just like you and I would do and this one call changes her whole life for a lifetime. Was answering this wrong number a right decision? Explore the answer as you read through her story.

Chap 1

DAY AT ADLABS

"Avani, let's go it's getting late; I don't want to miss the start, how much time you are taking to get ready?" called out Tanvi, as she put on her earrings.

"Yes Ma'am I'm done, let's go, I'm so excited. Chalo chalo lets move else we will get late", rushed Avani, picking up the keys. Both of them locked the flat and ran through the stairs not wanting to waste time for lift. Tanvi took scooty keys from Avani and they started for Adlabs.

Avani was a shy, homely, reserved—typical Maharashtrian girl, she was so much dependent on her parents when she was in school that her parents were much tensed to send her to Pune for education, where she was supposed to live in hostel and continue her studies. But their tension was a matter of few days as here she found Tanvi who was from Kerala, an independent girl determined to leave her footprints in this world by her work even after she was gone, Avani mirrored her thoughts and they both never left a chance to enjoy life. After meeting Tanvi, Avani's parents were relaxed that their daughter has found a good friend who was independent and could take care of herself. Avani got attached to Tanvi emotionally very soon as Tanvi had replaced her parents in those years, Avani would consult her for everything. They slowly started depending on each other. Live for today that was the mantra that they followed and they both were there for each other at time of need. They had been roommates since 1st year of engineering and they both were thankful for the college hostel for gifting them such a wonderful friend. Since then they had been together always. Avani being very much attached and dependent on her family often felt home sick in the beginning, but later Tanvi's company made her hostel sick. After completing engineering, both moved in Avani's flat in Kalyaninagar; one of the luxurious areas of Pune. Though their streams were different they were able to get placed through campus in the same company and now they were working for a MNC in Pune. Both had a lot common interests. Their daily routine was very busy, every morning they had to get up at 6 am and get ready for the office bus which would be at the door step sharp at 7:00 am, they would relax in the bus, once they would reach office the only thing that concerned them was their first cup of coffee, Avani was addicted to coffee if she would not have that cup of coffee for whole day she would have headache, Tanvi never skipped coffee with her, that would give her chance to start the day with smiles. There were couple of more friends who would join them for coffee; the topic of discussion would vary from current affairs to home affairs to leg pulling of someone in the group. After that they would go back to their desk and start work. Avani and Tanvi were in different projects and buildings, so the only time they used to be together was at tea and lunch break apart from the continuous chat on office communicator. Avani still had innocence alive in her, Tanvi would treat her like her younger sister and guide her in every step. Tanvi was mature enough to take her own decisions and she fought with her parents to come to Pune for education, they wanted her to get married, but today she was happy with her decision. In the evening when they would come back home, they would be so tired that Maggiee was their favorite meal many times not because of its taste but that was the simplest and easiest meal they could afford after a tiring day. Listening to news, watching their favorite show they would have Maggiee and in the end retire to their rooms. On weekends they would take full advantage to enjoy life, they had a plan for every weekend and this weekend was very special. Today, they were very much excited; not only because this was their first movie in the newly opened Adlabs multiplex but also because it was a comeback movie of their favorite hero. Tanvi had brought the tickets for the movie 3 days in advance to avoid the last minute curiosity. Tanvi and Avani were busy anticipating how the movie would be, unaware of what destiny had in store for them, they kept chatting all the way. Since they had just shifted to their new flat they were not very familiar with the route. Tanvi droved as per Avani's instruction which she gave her after querying people around for the route, mean time Avani told the live radio commentary to Tanvi.

"Hey Tannu, listen to this . . . your favorite track is being played on the radio!" and she unplugged one of her earphone and plugged it to Tanvi's ear.

"WOW! Sonu Nigam he is so sweet na . . . Chaha hai tuzhko . . . Tera milna paal do paal ka meri dhadkane. . . . la . . . laa . . . la . . ." Tanvi sang shaking her head on the rhythm of the song, just then they reached the multiplex.

There was rich crowd at multiplex, Tanvi dropped Avani at the entrance and moved to the parking area. She parked the scooty and hurried to the entrance. Avani was waiting for her there and desperately searching something in her purse. Tanvi went near her and said in desperation don't tell me you forgot to bring the tickets?

"Huh?" Avani gave a blank look to her and again continued with her search. After some time, when Tanvi felt the mood getting spoilt, she dragged Avani with her and gave the tickets to the door keeper. Avani was shocked and happy at same time.

"I knew u would forget to get them along, so I had already put them in my purse. Now come on don't search for explanations . . . you won't get any", said Tanvi smiling.

"But Tanuuu, I didn't forget the tickets. I didn't find them in the drawer when I went to get them so I was sure you picked it."

"Ohh yes you knew the tickets were with me and that is why you were looking for them in **your** purse, haa? Right?" Tanvi said raising her eyebrows and pinching Avani slightly. ummm . . . hmmm . . . Avani was bewildered and she cried in pain rubbing her arm where Tanvi pinched

"Let it be dear . . . it happens you don't need to explain. I know you are also so excited about all this", blinked Tanvi.

Avani felt relaxed and she too let it go. Again the air got excited. There was an escalator; Avani had never been on an escalator before. She was scarred to board it. Tanvi tried to distract her attention and drag her but she was reluctant.

"There is no other way to reach there? No, wait no, leave me I will fall. I can't come yaar . . . Tanuuu it's not that easy don't, don't you laugh dear." Avani was behaving like a small kid, not ready to listen to his mamma. Tanvi tried very hard to tell her it's not very difficult, "Avani . . . come on, it's not that dangerous, ok . . . see, think as if this is a steady staircase and you have to climb only one step and then stay there for a while? What say? Let's try? "

"No . . ." Avani replied depicting horror on her face, nervous she looked around for some other way and was dazed to see, because of her, all people had crowded behind them which only added to her embarrassment. Someone suggested stopping the escalator for a moment. She agreed to it and the escalator was stopped for the time she boarded it and then it again started. Now she felt good. She enjoyed the short ride but then again at the top she was scared to disembark; but Tanvi managed to distract her attention and make her get off the escalator at right time.

"Hush . . . thank God I'm safe!" Avani sighed as soon as she was off the escalator.

"As if you would have not reached the top, huh? You are such a cartoon you know. You were everyone's attraction there." Tanvi said teasing her and waving her hands at her.

"Yes. I know people were staring at me with wide eyes. But what can I do Tanuu if my leg would have got caught in between those STAIRS?" And she rolled her eyes in terror. As she scanned the surroundings she exclaimed in excitement, "Hey look there are so many nice stalls out there. Come we will do some window shopping." Avani called out Tanvi, who was laughing uncontrollably. There were different stalls. They both went to each one of them examining the material.

"Do you think these will go with my blue Salwar kameez?" Tanvi said showing a pair of earring to Avani.

"Which one, the one you stitched yesterday? "

"Yes won't they look pretty?"

"Umm yes they seem to be ok, but I liked these I think these will be better? What do you say?" Avani said showing her another pair of earring

"Ohh my my; they are so beautiful and it's a complete set of bracelet, earring, necklace, anklet and it's so cute, I liked it. I will buy this." Tanvi was happy to find the set.

The next shop was a shoe shop; they both sat there and were trying pair of sandals. Asking each other which was good and which suited more, latest design and all analysis was going on. They moved on to the other shop once the shopping there was done.

After a while they could see a guy coming towards them who was breathless, he came near to them and bowed down gasping some air, Tanvi and Avani looked at him puzzled. He was holding his stomach and then after a while he raised his hands towards Avani which had a wallet. Avani was surprised, she took it from him and thanked him, Tanvi gave her puzzled look with questions in her eyes like, "where did you forget it?"

"I found it at the door, saw your photo in it and by coincidence I saw you shopping at the first floor . . . so . . ." he stopped to gasp air.

"Ahh . . . you might have dropped it there when you were creating scene for the escalator . . ." Tanvi rolled her eyes.

"No, no . . . it was at the entrance door." clarified the guy.

"May be when I was searching for keys in my handbag I dropped it." Avani provided explanation with innocence.

"hmm right", said Tanvi and turning towards him she thanked him.

"Hi my name is Atharva . . . ." he gave his hand to her in anticipation of a handshake. Tanvi shook her head and said, "Hi, I'm Tanvi . . ." he seemed disappointed so Avani took his hand and did a shake hand and said, "Hi, I'm Avani and Thank you so much . . . for chasing me from ground floor just to return this wallet to me . . ." He was pleased and said, "welcome!!" greeting each other a bye they parted their ways.

"Avani, please be careful next time, it was your luck that you got your wallet back, thanks to that good fellow. And I have said so many times to you don't carry everything in your wallet, you have all your credit card, debit card, pan card and what not cards in your wallet, do you understand how much it could have cost you?" Tanvi roared at Avani warning her to be careful and signaled her to move, they kept on showing each other the minutest detail that excited them about the multiplex and which they found was something unique. After admiring the multiplex's architecture and the various stalls there (As by now you know, they left no stone unturn, Girls you know), they had shopped enough for themselves and they thought so because it was now time for the movie, meanwhile they had some sandwiches and sat on the chairs to make their feet relax a bit after that long shopping session.

"I think we did a good thing by coming early we got to see around and also shop I'm feeling so nice I got so many nice things. The purse I bought is so unique." Avani's face showed satisfaction.

"Yes. I also liked it but the lady had only one piece." Tanvi was disappointed.

"It's ok you can also use it sometime", grinned Avani.

"Ohh I don't need your permission for that; Anyways I'm taking it to office tomorrow. Hehehe" Avani too joined her in the laugh. Both started giggling as the doors opened and they were guided to their seat by the door keeper and then the most awaited moment came . . . The movie started. The first scene was a murder. Tanvi could not see that scene. She closed her eyes and tried to get a glimpse through gap in her fingers, then there was a song . . . where the titles rolled and they saw name of their favorite hero appearing and so on the movie continued they both got engrossed in the movie. In the interval Tanvi took out her phone and saw there were 4 missed calls, she looked for the number but it was an unknown number. She checked the profile, her phone was on silent, she changed her phone profile to ringing. If her parents would call and she would not pick the call they would unnecessarily get tensed, she thought to herself. She again checked the number, someone called her 4 times, but since her cell was on vibrator she did not realize, who it might be, she thought, then she thought whoever it is will call her again if needed, and since it is unknown number why should she bother, not paying much attention to it she took the popcorn from Avani, they chatted about the movie, how different it was from what they had seen in the trailers and all. Just then Tanvi received a call from the same unknown number. With hesitation she said "Hello."

"Is Ritu there?" said an unknown voice on the other side.

"Sorry?? Whom do u want to speak? There is no Ritu here, wrong number!" Tanvi disconnected the phone.

Avani was about to ask her about the call but then the movie started. So they both forgot about the call and they got engrossed in the movie. Sometime later again Tanvi's mobile started ringing in a high tone, feeling embarrassed she went out of the hall to get the call. She looked at the number it was the same unknown number, she answered it "Hello . . ."

"Hello, Is Ritu there I need to talk to her please I know she is there please connect me to her", said the desperate voice on the other side.

"I'm so sorry but this is not Ritu's number can you please check the number again. Probably you have dialed the Wrong Number", Tanvi answered politely and she rushed back to her seat, cursing the unknown fellow for making her miss the movie partly.

This happened for 2-3 times again. Tanvi really got frustrated now. She decided to be rude now. After all why should she every time leave her seat to attend a wrong number and miss shots, action scene of her favorite hero. Tanvi again changed her cell profile to silent and making it a point to scold this man she came back to her seat. Avani was already feeling uncomfortable.

"What's going on?" She signaled her.

"Aree, I don't know who this fellow is it's a wrong number, he is asking for some Ritu, I have told him so many times its not Ritu's number but he still keeps calling me . . ."

"Are you sure he is not any of your friend? May be someone playing prank?" Avani whispered.

"No . . . I don't remember listening to his voice." Tanvi said confused . . . "But you know what . . .", Avani signaled her to stop and pay attention to the movie now and tell her details later. As Tanvi had expected, the unknown number again flashed on her mobile screen. The movie was at its climax and getting very interesting she was determined to cut the call, but she thought maybe he has some urgent work with that girl. So reluctantly she answered the call, before the person said anything she started,

"Look Mr., I don't know who you are. I'm trying to be polite to you but let me tell you this isn't Ritu's number and I don't know any Ritu. Please check the number you have dialed. Please don't bother me again. I can't do anything if Ritu gave you this as her number. But in reality it's not Ritu's number it's my number so please excuse me." Tanvi said in one breath and was happy that she finally rudely told this fellow that she doesn't bother who Ritu he wants to talk to satisfied she was about to press the end call button when the voice on other end said, "Hi, this is Madhav and actually I wanted to talk to **you**." Tanvi was shocked but digesting her shock she said, "Me? why? Do I know you? Who Madhav?" Tanvi stressed her grey cells to recall, "Ammm ahhh I can't recollect if I know any Madhav."

"Can you spare 5 min I will let you know all details . . ." the voice on other side pleaded.

"ahh . . . what?? 5 min . . . ohh any ways ok . . . we can talk but not now please call me after 15-20 min." saying this she turned to go to her seat but on the screen in bold letters she could only see written

The Beginning!!

Chap 2

The Mysterious Call

Tanvi was sad as she missed the end but her curiosity was on verge to know who this unknown caller was. Tanvi and Avani started moving towards parking while Avani narrated the movie end to her.

Now your turn said Avani finishing her story narration. Tanvi gave a puzzled look.

"So who was it, for whom you missed the movie? Who was it whom you could not say no and answered the call every time he called? Whom you gave priority over Mr. Khan?"

"Aree yaar even I don't know who it was; it was a wrong number."

"Ohh I didn't know people call on wrong number for nth time? Huh?? You think I'm a fool?"

"Believe me Avani, I don't know why I answered him every time but . . . and yes it was a **wrong number.** Now let's not argue about it and move for dinner, I'm very hungry." Tanvi declared as she unlocked the scooty.

They went to a nearby restaurant; making themselves comfortable. They were chatting about the movie,

"I don't like the fighting scenes usually but in this it was very funny to watch the fight." Avani declared.

"Ya I know it was a good movie. I liked the terrace scene, how he jumps to save the chickens and . . ." Tanvi took out her cell and before she could complete her sentence she saw there were 4 missed calls. A discomfort was seen on her face, noting that Avani could not help but ask what's the matter? Tanvi showed her the mobile and Avani in disbelief rolled her eyes.

"Do you recollect talking to him earlier? I'm sure he might be some school friend or from your college? Why would someone call so many times on a wrong number?" Avani asked Tanvi to recall.

"Huh? No yaar, though his voice was very attention seeking, I mean he had a sexy manly voice. If I would have talked to him earlier I wouldn't forget that voice."

Tanvi's phone started ringing. Even Tanvi was getting curious about this unknown person.

"Hello", she answered with lots of questions reflecting in her voice.

"Hi Ritu, this is Madhav, ohh sorry but till now you are Ritu for me, you haven't told me your other name. I know you might be wondering what's going on. This person was asking for Ritu and then he says he wants to talk to me."

"Umm . . . **yes!!** I'm Tanvi and this is my only name not my **other** name", said Tanvi in stubborn voice.

"**Tanvi,** Tanvi is also a nice name, cute better than Ritu", and he started laughing to himself. "Actually, I can guess peoples name, personality, and their likes and dislikes without actually seeing them, but only by listening their voice! When I heard your voice I knew your name should start with 'R' and I thought it should be Ritu."

"But I'm not Ritu!"

"Yes got it. So do you want to know what all I know about you even without seeing you."

"Yes, go ahead I'm all ears."

"Umm from my guess you should be 5+ feet tall, medium build with dark thick long hair and a golden complexion."

Tanvi was shocked. Being from Kerala she did have long dark hair and she was 5.5 feet tall everything was so correct. She was thinking about herself for the first time so seriously. Her thought process was broken by the waiter who came there to get the order. Avani asked her, what she would like to have. She signaled her anything will do.

"Hello? Tanvi you there? What happened?" said Madhav who was waiting for her answer.

"Hmm yes, you sound interesting. You know so much about me already let me know something about you."

"Me?? Umm I'm an open book. I work the whole day and in evening when I feel like talking to a friend I dial a random number and make friends. Today it was your turn to be my friend so I dialed your number."

"Hmm, quite a new way of exploring the world; so how many friends have you made like this?"

"Many, at least one get added to the list every month. And now you are also added in the list."

"Hey, wait a sec I never said we are friends! How can you just take it granted?"

"Ohhh is that so, I know what you might be thinking but we will never meet, I just want to make friends. We will always be Phone friend. Now is that fine? I will call you only when you are free. Only when you say we can talk; I won't trouble you, come on yaar, even I have work, just thought, better to clarify so that you don't start building the road side Romeo types image of me", and he laughed. "So? I hope that should not be any problem. If you still feel you don't want to go ahead with this friendship proposal I promise I won't trouble you again, but I think you should give this a chance and I will prove you how good friend I am." he paused for her answer.

"Hmm ok. I'm saying yes to this only because I don't want to disappoint you. You called me so many times with lot of hope! **AND"** she stressed her words . . . **"We will never meet."** By this time the dinner was ready and served, Avani was already feeling alone. Knowing this Tanvi said to Madhav, "We will talk later; I'm having my dinner now."

"Yes, sure, thanks for talking, I felt very nice. I will call you tomorrow. Is evening time ok with you? Around 8-8:30 pm?"

"Ok. I will be waiting!" saying that she disconnected the call.

Avani had a thousand questions in her mind waiting for the call to complete. Looking at Avani Tanvi said, "I'm so sorry for keeping you waiting."

"What's going on madam?" questioned Avani, raising her eyebrows.

"I will tell you everything once we reach our flat. Ok? Now can we have dinner in peace?" Tanvi pleaded. "Hmm this curry is delicious, isn't it?"

"After all whose choice it is", said Avani raising her imaginary collar.

After finishing dinner they went home. Whole way Avani bugged Tanvi but Tanvi was adamant let's reach home first. As soon as they were in the flat, Avani threw all her shopping bags, purse and jumped on the sofa, "So?? Now tell me what happened? What did he say?? How is he?? What did you talk for so long?"

One question at a time ma'am . . .

"Tanuu you are trying my patience now. I don't want to listen to your stupid conversation. Forget it I'm going to sleep."

"Ohh my baby got angry . . . ok listen, his name is **Madhav**. It is his hobby to call random numbers."

"Calling random numbers? Isn't it a strange hobby? And from where did he get your number."

"He makes friends like that. And I told na, random number, he might have just dialed any number that came to his mind."

"And . . . What else? You talked so long." Avani was getting curious.

"He said he can tell ones nature personality just by listening to his voice. He just wants to be friend with me and he will call me in evenings."

"What did u say?"

"Ok."

"OK?? You mean now you will talk to a **straaanger**? It's not good, it's not safe Tannu."

"You are somewhat right but he said he will never ask me to meet. So what's the harm in just being a phone friend? And I have just spoken with him for some few minutes. If I find it's not good to talk to him or it's not safe I can always quit. But shouldn't we give this friendship a chance? So I said its ok with me, he can call me tomorrow evening. From his 1st impression I felt he is a good person."

"What made you feel he is a good person?"

"He talked in a very polite manner. His voice was confident enough to convince me he is not the wrong person. Actually I liked his name . . . I know that is a foolish reason. But when he told me his name I just could not say no to him. I don't know, argued Tanvi. "Chalooo lets sleep now. It's already very late. You are already yawning."

Both went to sleep, deep in their thoughts. Tanvi still kept thinking about her conversation with Madhav. Thinking how he could tell peoples' personality just by listening to their voice. Where was he from? What does he do? All such questions kept creeping in her mind. To every question she had only one answer—I will ask him tomorrow. Sometime later she went to sleep, waiting for the new dawn in her life.

Chap 3

The Surprise

No matter what they tell us . . . What we believe is true . . . If only tears were laughter . . . If only prayers were answers . . . then we won't hear God say . . . And I will keep you safe and strong and shelter from the storm . . . No matter . . . was playing in the background. Tanvi and Avani were busy in household chores, Avani was preparing tea and Tanvi was reading newspaper. The day went by as just another day.

In the evening Madhav called Tanvi, Tanvi was waiting for his call. She was excited to know her new friend. The whole concept of Phone friend was exciting for her. They talked a lot about everything. They talked about how their day was, their likes, dislikes. Their favorite pastime, Tanvi learned that Madhav liked reading books, movies and chatting. Tanvi told him she liked gardening, movies, trekking and she has been to some places in and near pune with her friends for trekking like lonavala, khandala . . . She told him her experiences of trek. Once she was about to fall from a rock, where she stood to get a picture. How she was followed by monkeys when they went to

Lohagad . . . they kept on chatting. He told her some funny incidents. Time kept ticking and it was very late. They said goodnight to each other and disconnected the phone.

"Ohhh noooo my battery is down", Said Tanvi surprised . . . I had charged it yesterday only . . . there was disappointment in her voice.

"If you talk for 2-3 hours continuously on phone off course the battery will discharge", Avani said sarcastically.

"Hmm yes that's true", Tanvi said mischievously, "someone is J" and she hopped on the bed.

"What J? Why should I feel jealous? He is not a superstar that I should feel jealous that he is your friend. This whole concept is wrong, roared Avani. Ok, jokes apart, now are you going to tell me what happened? Who is he? What does he do? Where is he from?"

"Hmmm see even you are curious to know about him", teased Tanvi.

"Yes I'm, cause . . . cause . . . my best friend . . ."

"Umm ok . . . ok . . . let it be . . . I understand" Tanvi smiled back, putting on the radio which played . . ." yaroo dosti . . . badi hi haseen hai . . . ye na ho toh . . . kya phir . . . koi toh ho razdaaar . . . , see the song is so apt . . . whom else will I tell, if not you. He is from Mumbai but is staying in Pune. He stays in Shivajinagar. He loves watching movies, reading novels and is a big chatter box. Whole time he was describing funny incidents."

"You found it funny?? I think it's a game he is playing with you? You should be careful . . . don't get involved into him."

"Ohh come on Avani I'm just speaking to him . . . getting involved and all is far away . . . This is all so much excitement . . . I have a friend whom I haven't seen but still I know so much about him . . . just imagine!! He is a nice guy . . . I feel you should also talk to him . . . Ya your advice is taken . . . I will be careful . . . happy?"

"I don't need such imaginary friends I have enough friends. So what does he do? What's his age? Is he younger to you?"

"Ummm??? Huh?? We were busy talking on more serious topics I didn't ask him these questions. He has promised me he will call me tomorrow. I will ask him at that time . . . ok?"

Time went on . . . every day Madhav called Tanvi . . . Tanvi use to feel good after talking to him. All her office worries, tensions she would tell him and he would always give her good suggestions. She wondered if she actually bored him but then she would let that thought go saying if he would have been bored he won't call her. She was very impressed by his convincing and speaking skills. He would solve all her problems so quickly. How can someone put one at ease without being with them? Then she would recollect, He is a lawyer . . . he knows how to handle critical situations well. But he never talks about his work pressure. He is so cool. How can someone be so cool? These questions kept troubling her she use to decide to ask him next day . . . and next day Madhav use to talk on something else . . . she would just keep listening to it. She felt as if she was listening to some music . . . she never argued to him on any matter he used to put forth his point so well. Their friendship was growing every day. Tanvi used to wait impatiently for his calls. Avani talked to him 2-3 times; even she stopped resisting Tanvi from talking to him. Avani also liked him. It had been three months they were talking to each other. They knew each other very well . . . then one day Madhav called her as usual,

"Hi, what is going on? Had dinner? How was your day today?"

"There is something special today! Want to take some guess?" Tanvi said

"Umm you got promotion?"

"No, you can give one more try"

"Haa, your parents are visiting?"

"No Madhav, it's very special; someone made it a very special day."

"Oh! You mean you met somebody? May be your dream boy? Ha? Caught you right?"

"No dumbo, you are useless fellow, today is a great day, because, today is my **Birthday**."

"Ohhh! Is it?? So what all things did you do?? You should have told me earlier na, this is not fair, I would have called you in the morning yaar."

"Do you want to know how full of suspense my day was . . . hehehe . . . I had so many surprises today."

"Yes, sure please go on, I'm very eager to know how your day went"

"You know what, at 12 a.m. a delivery boy delivered a cake for me written Happy B'day! Then I and Avani celebrated my B'day cutting the cake . . . early morning I got a bouquet of red and white roses delivered. It was so cute Madhav. They are still looking fresh. I received so many surprises today. Then we got a call from Esquare, They said, they have sent two tickets of the current running block buster movie—Anjane, It's Arjun's movie, you remember na Madhav . . . I like him so much. I enquired a lot to them about who has booked them for me and how they got to me . . . but they said they are not supposed to disclose **his** name."

"So did you enjoy the movie?"

"Yes Madhav, I loved the movie it was a full on comedy movie, after I got that call from Esquare I took off from office. I went with Avani for the movie. Then after that we shopped for some time then in the evening we had dinner at my favorite restaurant. It was such a coincidence, there all my favorite songs were being played, Boyzone and backstreet boys . . . Quit playing games with my heart . . . I liked the evening a lot. After having dinner we returned home . . . on the door there was a bunch of Tuberose waiting for me . . . with a sweet anonymous note . . . "Hope you enjoyed your day." I'm full tired right now . . . But my room is still filled with the freshness that these flowers have brought in.

"What happened next?"

"Next I'm talking to you . . ." Then there was a silence for few minutes, long one. "Thanks a lot Madhav . . . You made my day!! I have never got so many surprises ever in my life. How did you come to know it's my B'day I don't remember telling you, and how did you plan everything so perfect. It was a very big Big BIG surprise. Thanks a lot."

"Why are you thanking me? What have I done?"

"Come on now I know it's all you're planning. Just tell me how did you do all this?"

"How did you come to know?"

"Nobody other than you and Avani knows about me in so much detail. Esquare people said they cannot disclose his name and it came to my mind right now. So now tell me how did you got these ideas . . . how did you come to know it's my B'day."

"That day when I talked to Avani, I had asked her about your B'day. Then I planned all this with her. She only told me that you love surprises. There is still one surprise pending. I sent those flowers, cake and movie."

"OMG you are so sweet Madhav. Thanks, I just can't express what all this means to me. Thanks a lot again. I had a great day. Thank you."

"OK. Chalo then have a nice sleep. May the whole year go in getting pleasant surprises . . . hahaha . . . And . . . **Happy B'day . . . to you . . . happy bday to you . . . may GOooD bless you . . .** Madhav started singing for Tanvi, May all your wishes come true Tanvi . . . Happy Bday!! I think I'm not late its still 2 min to go for 12. Bye."

They both wished each other good night and disconnect the call. Tanvi looked outside the window, The Moon was shining bright and the stars were twinkling, the atmosphere was very beautiful and ideal for a walk in moonshine. Neglecting the feeling She went in switched on the radio, Nothings gonna change my love for you . . . the radio started singing, listening to it Tanvi went into deep thoughts . . .

He remembered my favorite color . . . so he sent me red and white roses. Even the cake was so sweet . . . rainbow colored. He remembered my favorite hero . . . my type of movie . . . he got me the movie tickets . . . of Arjun's "Anjane" . . . He remembered everything that I told him . . . Till now I thought Avani took me to my favorite restaurant, but now I know Madhav told her . . . he had planned all my favorite music there. He made sure I enjoy every sec of my day. He sent those bunch of tuberose . . . my room is still fresh.

Lost in his thought she hopped on her bed and went to sleep still thinking about Madhav, just then she felt there was something below her pillow. She pulled it out . . . it was a B'day card . . . OMG . . . she thought to herself as she remembered Madhav saying last surprise is still pending. She opened it. There was a very sweet message carved in the card. She read each word with great affection and in the end the "from" name read **Madhav**. A tear rolled out from her eye. How much can someone care!! She thought to herself. "Madhav, there was only one thing missing . . . she said imagining him, as if he was sitting in front of her, It would have been so much fun if you could join with us. I wish that day comes soon . . . Thanks" she closed her eyes . . . And there in the sky the Angels said **Amen**.

Chap 4

THE ANSWERED PRAYER

Tanvi started from office early that day. Her friend Riya was coming. They had decided to meet at FC road, CCD. Tanvi being time punctual reached CCD at 5 and waited for Riya. FC road is all time crowded place, she spent time looking at people, just then she heard a familiar voice.

"Excuse me, I had reserved a table here", said the voice at the CCD counter. Tanvi could not hold her anxiousness; she walked up to the counter and curiously watched that person, "May I know by what name the table is booked sir?" questioned the receptionist politely.

". . . Madhav . . ." said the voice firmly, Tanvi skipped a heart beat; her heart was beating faster and faster. She looked at him or rather starred at him. She was not aware what she did, she was happy or she was not. Madhav walked and went to the table the receptionist pointed to. While Tanvi kept looking at him as he strode to the table smiling back at the receptionist and thanking her, his smile was so innocent. As he sat there she watched him. He was waiting for someone, she thought. Perplexed Tanvi stood there, thinking if she should go and confirm if He is the same Madhav she had longed to meet, his deep blue eyes were inviting her. Without giving a second thought she started towards his table, He was busy with his cold coffee that had just arrived. Looking at the cold coffee she smiled to herself thinking they were so much similar, it was chilling cold outside and even she felt like having a cold coffee instead of a hot steaming coffee. She stood there for a while appreciating him silently. After a while Madhav looked at her, their eyes met . . . with questions in his eyes he uttered "Excuse me? May I help you?" Bewildered Tanvi shook her head and Madhav again got lost in his coffee. She then with a weak voice called out Madhavvvv? Is that you? With hope to get an affirmative answer.

On hearing Tanvi's voice Madhav raised his head in a flash of light and said, "Tanviii; you here? How come?" "OMG, they both exclaimed . . . It's such a pleasure to meet you. Please have a seat", exclaimed Madhav as he pulled out a chair adjacent and offered her.

"Yes sure." Tanvi agreed chirpily.

"So what brought you here? I'm still shocked; all of a sudden I meet my phone friend. This has never happened to me . . . It's a big surprise for me", said Madhav in disbelief.

"Ya I know, if I would have not heard you at the counter may be I would have not recognized you. Actually my office colleague is coming from Mysore today in Pune and we decided to meet here", explained Tanvi.

"Ohhh I never knew you have such great fans even at work, that they come to meet you from Mysore?" Madhav gave her a mischievous look.

Tanvi replied him with a question mark.

"What I mean is . . . I'm a fan of you outside workplace . . . and thought to be your only fan . . . but now I came to know you have fans all over the world."

Tanvi blushed on that and started reasoning hmmm . . . "She was in Pune earlier and we are good friends then she got transferred to Mysore, she is getting engaged next month. She has come here for shopping. She wants me to accompany her."

"You girls just need reason for shopping. She came from Mysore, to do wedding shopping?? And it's her engagement next month. I'm sure her engagement shopping might have already finished 2 months back . . . ohh no . . . no no . . . does girls shopping ever end??" Madhav was shaking his head as if he was in full agreement with himself.

Tanvi hit him with her hand bag. "It's long time she should have been here", said Tanvi in a worried tone and she took out her mobile to check. "No wonder; my mobile battery was low and it's switched off now. Riya might be trying my number." Tanvi's voice got tensed.

Madhav looked around and he found a charging point, pointing in the direction he asked Tanvi to charge her cell there and mean while she could call her friend from his cell. Tanvi liked the idea; she called up Riya from Madhav's cell.

"Hello?" Came the reply

"Hi Riya, this is Tanvi. I'm calling from my friends mobile, Where are you? I'm waiting for you in CCD 1st floor."

"Tanuu, I'm caught in a bad traffic jam here; it will take another hour to reach FC. Can you wait? I tried your cell 2-3 times."

"My mobile battery is dead. You can call me on this number if needed. Ya I will wait, you try making it quick."

"Ya, sure will try to make it early, bye."

"Bye!", said Tanvi and disconnected the call. I hope you are free for next hour; "I will need to spend another one hour here." She is caught up in a traffic jam, said Tanvi returning his cell to Madhav.

"Any time for you, I'm always free, it's ok with me to wait another hour", smiled Madhav "and that will give me chance to spend time with you", grinned Madhav.

"Your parents might be waiting at home."

"I don't have anyone waiting for me, I live alone here. Tanvi there's something I wanted to tell you, but I could never tell. I have lied to you."

"What?? Tanvi said in disbelief with 100 thoughts processing in background."

"I'm not a lawyer", said Madhav with a weak voice, nervousness showing up in his voice. "I know you hate lies. I tried telling this to you many times but I could not correct the mistake that I did. When you asked me my profession, I thought might be you won't like it and that time I was watching a court scene, so nothing else came to my mind at that moment."

"Then . . ." asked Tanvi with a voice filled with anxiety "what do you do?"

"I'm an officer in merchant navy. Girls usually are not much attracted to these fields. But I was bought up watching the sea. I was the most privileged boy in the orphanage; from my bedside window I could see the sea view."

"ORPHANAGE??" questioned Tanvi with wide eyes.

"Yes, I'm brought up in an orphanage in Mumbai; I have been in Mumbai since when it was Bombay. I have not seen my parents. My mentor told me they died in an accident. I was a bright student; I completed my studies with the help of various scholarships that I bagged. When I turned 18 it was time for me to leave the orphanage. I had only one relation in my life from childhood, relation with the Sea. I used to talk with her for hours, whenever I was sad I use to go to the shore sit there and after some time my heart use to feel at peace. I went to sleep listening "lories" that the waves sung for me. The waves were my alarm clock. As I grew I built a boat for myself. I loved going deep into the sea I felt as if my Mom is hugging me. The fishes and dolphins in sea became my friends."

"WOW!! I love Dolphins." Tanvi exclaimed as she continued to listen to him.

"I decided to opt for merchant navy. That way I will never be away from my first love. There was no doubt of rejection. I had prepared with full determination and yes I got selected."

"Then you left the orphanage?"

"Yes. That's the rule when you are 18; they leave you to face the world alone. As a parting gift they gifted me a mobile; but, whom will I call? I had no one in world to call. So I started dialing random numbers, got weird experiences with people. Some will ignore you and some will be friendly with you. I made many such friends and I haven't met any of them till today except you."

"Seriously, Really?? I can't believe this."

"Hmm I know it's strange. But for me voice has become the primary identification of a person. I have been listening to the waves and I know when the sea is angry and when calm. Similarly I can guess the persons personality by voice. In this crowd I don't know people by face. But I know there are people in the same crowd whom I know by their voice. This crowd no more seems unfamiliar to me. I feel I know each one of them personally."

"I had disconnected the call 4-5 times still you kept calling me why?? You had that much confidence that I will talk to you??"

"There was something in your voice that gave me hope. I didn't want to lose on my hope to gain a good friend so I called you again, and see we are such good friends now."

"Hmm yes, I'm happy you kept trying else I would have also not found such a good friend."

"Hi Tannu . . ." came a weak hi, from behind. It was Riya; she looked tired by the long travel. "I'm so sorry!! When will Pune traffic get better yaar . . ." complained Riya.

"Hey Riya, come have a sit. Finally you reached. Ohh its 1 ½ hr I called you yaar. Anyways, meet my friend Madhav. I had called you from his mobile and I could wait such a long only because of him."

Madhav and Riya greeted each other. Riya had a cup of hot cappuccino, which refreshed her spirits. Riya showed them her fiancés photo, talked about her plans and stay in Pune. They got so well mixed up they forgot about time. After some more chit chatting and fun when Tanvi saw the watch it was 7 P.m.

"OMG Riya lets move yaar, I guess we won't be able to shop much today. I even have office tomorrow."

"If you don't mind, I can come along with you. I have a car, which can reduce your time for searching an auto, we can drive to the mall and then I can drop you both home."

Both of them agreed to the offer. As Pune's auto drivers . . . you know ahhh . . . They went to mall shopped, ate. Madhav participated actively in their shopping gave lot of suggestions, helped them in choosing. At 10 P.M. they went to restaurant had dinner, then Madhav dropped Riya at her place.

On the drive to Tanvi's place, "Kathaiy aankhon wali ek ladki . . . ek hi baat pe bighadti hai . . . tum muzhe kyu nahi mile pehle . . . roz ye kehkar muzhse ladti hai . . ." was playing on radio in background.

"Tannuu . . . I mean Tanvi . . . It was nice meeting you. It was a great surprise, pleasant surprise I must say. You are as exciting person as you sound on phone."

"Thanks and Tannu is ok with me . . . all my friends call me Tannu . . . u too can call me Tannu", smiled back Tanvi.

"Tannu I know this might sound a bit odd . . . Actually your friend came else I would have told this to you today itself . . . I want to tell you one more thing . . . Can we meet tomorrow?? Same time same place? I mean only if it's ok with you. I'm not forcing you, but since it's important and even urgent. I would be more than happy if you accept."

"OK . . . No problem I will come to CCD at 5 tomorrow! But don't be late, I hate late comers."

Just then they reached Tanvi's place. Avani was worried for her. She was standing in the balcony waiting for her. Tanvi got down and went upstairs; she came to the balcony and as expected Madhav was waiting for her. She waved bye to him. After confirming she reached safely, Madhav drove off to his home. Tanvi kept on thinking what is that important thing for which Madhav has called her tomorrow to meet.

Chap 5

The Growing Friendship-I

12:30 A.M. showed the clock.

"Where have you been Tannuuu . . . I was so worried. You didn't even inform me. Who was that person who dropped you? Are you fine? Did you have dinner?" Tanvi was fired with questions from Avani.

"Relax Avani . . . I'm fine. Riya is in Pune. She wanted me to come along for her wedding shopping. So I went to CCD to meet her. And Avani you won't believe whom I met there."

"Who did you meet?" Avani asked plainly.

"I met Maddy . . ." Tanvi answered excitedly.

"Who is this?"

"Aree Madhav . . . I met Madhav in CCD."

"What . . ." Avani said in disbelief. "How is he?? How does he look? What was he doing there? What were you doing there? What did he say?" Continued Avani's firing.

"He stays in Shivajinagar na . . . he often goes to FC road CCD to relax, He is so sweet . . . When I saw him, the first thing that captured my attention were his **deep blue** eyes, they are as deep as the sea; don't know how much pain is hidden behind those big blue watery eyes. You know he is in merchant navy; that military cut with a cute smile. When he smiles na . . . his tooth peeps out, adding beauty to his smile. Tall, dark handsome, a dashing personality any girl would die for; and to top it he is so mannered he offered to come with us for Riya's shopping, He has a perfect taste, he helped us get the best in very short time, and his communications skills . . . you are already aware of . . . You know he loves sea . . . and He is not a **lawyer** . . . He . . . is . . ."

"What? Then he lied o you? Then what did you do?" Avani interrupted Tanvi's description.

"Actually when he was telling me I got so emotionally involved that I forgot he lied to me and . . . that he has done something wrong . . . That I hate liars . . . I don't know I didn't felt like I should be angry . . . or it was something great to be angry . . . ."

"What emotional story he told you? I was so worried about you. Tannuu watch out . . . I'm really worried for you."

Tanvi told Avani his complete story. How he got scholarships and how he completed his studies. How he managed on his own at a tender age of 18 . . . .

"You know his first call to unknown number was dialed to a Thief . . . They both talked for hours. Though Maddy could not be in touch with him for long as he might have changed his no . . . Still he is a good friend of his . . . and . . . eeeeeeee shouted Tanvi looking at the watch it showed 2:30 a.m Avani, We have office tomorrow . . . Let's sleep now . . . and they went to sleep."

Next Day evening . . . .

Tanvi felt from office as if she was waiting for this moment to come since ages . . . though it was just a matter of a day. She was lost in her thoughts when Madhav came, just in time said Tanvi to herself and kept smiling. They greeted each other and ordered their drinks, cold coffee in the cold weather.

"So tell me what is it? I'm so curious to know what is it that you wanted me to meet you."

"Yes, this is very important Tanvi . . . I'm here for next week, and then I need to go back on duty. I was here for vacations."

"Vacations, what do you mean?" Tanvi got a bit serious.

"Yes, we have jobs in 6 months slot. For 6 months I'm completely into Sea, sometimes I don't even get to see land, then for next 6 months I get to rest. It was this rest period that I was in Pune. I have to join my crew next week. I will be leaving for Mumbai and then maybe I won't be able to talk to you for next 6 months."

"Huh?? What are you saying?", Came the surprise expression.

"I should have told all this to you, I know but since I could not tell you my actual profession I could not tell you these details. Believe me I never wanted to hide anything about me. All my friends know about my job and its schedule. I don't know how you will take this but believe me I didn't do it hurt you . . . I know how I spend those 6 months without being in touch with any of my friend its really difficult but you know na why I opted for this job, I never wanted to hide anything from you . . . but . . ."

"Hmm hush" came a sigh from Tanvi. She did not say a word for 5 min. She kept stirring her coffee cup and starring at the formations in the cup. That only increased Madhav's tension

"Kehna hi kya yeh nain ek anjaan se jo mile . . . arman naye jo aise dil mein khile jinko kabhi main na janu . . . who humse hum unse kabhi na mile kaise mile dil na janu . . ." was playing in soft tune in the background while Tanvi was lost, she came back from her imaginary world when Madhav continued his explanation to convince her.

"Tannu . . . I know you hate lies. Tannu . . . I promise not to lie from now . . . forgive me this time. Please speak for God's sake. What are you thinking? Speak it aloud. If you want you can punish me. But let me tell you. I'm here only for next week, and then I won't be here for next 6 months. **Tannu . . .** are you listening to me?"

"Umm **yes**! I was planning for next week she replied to him . . ."

"What?" came sudden surprise expression from Madhav as if he received a 440 volt shock. He had expected to get . . . what not . . . but hearing Tanvi's reply he was happy . . . "So what have you decided let me know." Madhav said changing the topic and setting the jolly mood.

"Aaaa haaa . . . that's a surprise now . . . tell me what all places have you visited in Pune? Are you free tomorrow? Or you have meeting with other friends?"

Madhav was completely baffled. What was he supposed to answer . . . he was confused, excited, curious about the surprise . . . all at a time. He only jumped with joy . . . said thank you to Tanvi and said "I will call you later . . ." He left with his heart jumping in joy, joy of Tanvi forgiving him and accepting him as he is.

After reaching home . . . Tanvi and Avani both got busy deciding for next week's plan, They booked tickets for a movie . . . this time Madhav's favorite one . . . Tanvi had planned out something special for him for each evening. She wanted to get a special gift for him. She had so many things planned to do and such a less time. Tanvi had 5 days with her; Then Madhav would be leaving for Mumbai, where he would be doing his further preparations. Tanvi wanted these 5 evenings of Madhav's life to be the best, memorable. She was very hurt after knowing his life story. She wanted to give him all the joy that she could. She wanted him to believe there was someone who was waiting for his return, who cared for his happiness. These five days were the last hope she had and she wanted to give her best to him, best memories of friendship of his life. She initially thought of taking leave from office and to spend whole time with Madhav, but it was not possible to get leave for a week her work was getting hectic. She was sad but did not lose hope; she planned for the best evenings with Madhav. Whatever she could do for him, She wanted to make him feel important and cared. She wanted to make him realize how nice she feels to have a friend like him in her life, how she valued their friendship and how good he is as a person, as a friend.

Evening 1

Tanvi went to Madhav's place. She was all prepared to give him surprises . . . She carried a beautiful bouquet of Yellow roses with her, remembering his favorite color; which also had a beautiful card which said . . .

"I swear to you . . . I will always be *there for you* . . . Forever we will be together . . . More I get to know you . . . the more I care . . . with all of my heart you know I will always be there . . . Nothing can compare . . . I will always be . . . RIGHT THERE . . ."

After reading the card Madhav got a bit sentimental . . . "This means a lot for me Tannu . . . I have never received a surprise like this. Thanks."

"Dosti ka ek vasul hota hai Mr. No sorry no Thank you" Tanvi said imitating Bhagyashree from Maine Pyaar kiya making the song Tum ladki ho . . . main ladka hoon . . . aaya mausam Dosti ka play in back of their minds!! Then she rubbed her nose and continued. "No formalities, you are special friend of mine, and Tannu very well knows how to treat her friends . . ." giggled Tannu.

"So what next . . . ?" Madhav liked the royal treatment he was getting.

"Wait . . . Today you are going to have dinner with me . . . special dinner; Dinner prepared by World famous Chef Miss . . . Tannu!" came the reply as she bowed down to him.

"Ohh is it, but Chef sahiba, are you sure I will join the crew after having that special dinner?"

"Ahhhh . . . Whatttt did you say?? You mean . . . huh . . ." Tanvi said, hitting Madhav with the pillow kept on the sofa.

"Oouch oouch . . . Tannu it hurts . . . ok ok . . . lets decide it after you prepare dinner . . . I don't want to die hungry . . . you can kill me latter . . . ok . . . ok . . ."

Tanvi prepared the dinner. Right at the time when they were about to have dinner lights went . . . "hmm it seems we need to have candle light . . . this was not included in my plan . . ." grinned Tannu . . . shifting the table to terrace with Madhav . . . while Madhav kept smiling . . . "Even God want's to help you . . . hahaha . . ."

They both got everything settled; it was wonderful to have dinner under sky with moonlight and candles to add special effect. Madhav praised Tanvi for making a good dinner. Tanvi also thanked him for his help. After dinner they went outside to have a walk as there were no lights . . . .

"Maddy . . . , I always saw this full moon from window in my bedroom and thought of having a walk in moonlight but never actually got a chance . . . Its feeling like a dream come true . . . this soft wet grass touching out feet . . . the stars . . . they all seem so new . . . so different . . . I never knew such small things do matter in life."

"Hmm yes . . . I know God has already provided us with lot of things to be at peace but we don't even care to take a look at them."

"Hey it's getting late let me drop you at your home." Madhav took the car keys, Lets move . . . on the drive sweet songs played on the CD player . . . this time all of his favorites like Feel my love . . . Though Tanvi didn't get the meaning she liked the song . . . Madhav dropped Tanvi to her place and left . . . He was on his way when his cell beeped . . . he checked his cell it was Tanvi's msg,

Let's meet at Eqsuare tomorrow at sharp 6 PM. GN.
—Tannu.

Madhav smiled to himself and drove back to home.

Evening 2

They both met at ESquare. Tanvi was waiting for Madhav at the entrance, As soon as she saw him approaching; she welcomed him with a wide smile. As he reached he apologized for getting late. "I had flat tyre and so had to get the tyre changed. I'm sorry"

Tanvi tried to give him an angry look, but she could not help, she just could not get angry with him. She tried to act as if she was angry but Madhav was good in reading truth in her eyes.

"I thought you will get mad, I didn't even give my tyre for puncture repair, and it is lying in the dikki . . . Now if while going back we have a flat tyre, you are not supposed to get mad at me" he grinned declaring his innocence.

Tanvi smile back and pulled him to the theater. The movie was a comedy one and they enjoyed it to fullest, they laughed till it hurt their stomach, after the movie they started for a dinner. Madhav loved sea food . . . Tanvi took him to the 'Nisarg' the best sea food restaurant. Madhav liked the food quality there. After having food to their hearts content they moved on to *Naturals* to have ice-cream, there without any hesitation he ordered for two Roasted Almonds; Tanvi was surprised how he could know she wanted to have that flavor.

"Ohh, the other day you told me, you love Roasted Almond. You forgot?"

"Umm . . . forget it . . ." Tanvi said neglecting the thought licking her ice-cream.

While they were on their drive to Tanvi's home, Tanvi put on the radio;

". . . and now . . . we have a special request dedicated to Madhav and it is requested by Tanvi . . . Soo Tanvi and Madhav hope you are having great fun . . . Enjoy . . .

"Diye jalte hai . . . phool khilte hai . . . Badi mushkil se magar Duniya main Dost milte hai . . . played on the radio . . ."

Chap 6

THE GROWING FRIENDSHIP-II

Evening 3

Tanvi had planned to take Madhav to '**Manas Resort**'. It was a wonderful evening . . . Sun was about to set . . . sunrays filled up the Sky . . . Kissing the earth . . . They both enjoyed boating for initial 2 hours in the lake, chit chatting . . . watching other couples . . . passing comments and enjoying the beautiful nature that surrounded them . . . then they went go-carting . . . They many times dashed into each other . . . they had completely spoiled their clothes by now . . . but none of them was bothered about it. They enjoyed to the fullest. After go-carting they rocked the dance floor, they danced till they dropped on the floor. After enjoying so much, their feet were hurting and stomach was ringing alarm for food after every 2 mins finally they decided to have rest for a while and then they had dinner in peace. They took their plates and went in the lawn, besides the lake they took a corner table and enjoying the serenity they had food. The lake had soft waves going around; some couples still enjoying the boating; Tanvi and Madhav had dinner and talked for long. The moonlight made their face glow and they kept looking at the special glow lost in each other. They had so many things to talk about. The topics never end. They were tired and the soft breeze flowing did not make them feel like leaving the place, but it was very late and Tanvi had her office next day, reluctantly she agreed to leave for home. Madhav dropped her home . . . As usual she went to terrace . . . and bid good bye to Madhav . . . After making sure she has reached safely . . . Madhav drove back to his home . . . he increased the volume of radio, "Aree re aree ye kya huwa . . . Hum main tum main kuch toh hai . . . kuch nahi hai kya . . ." was playing on the radio . . . Madhav got lost in the rhythm shaking his head and anticipating next day he reached home. He was so tired that he slept right when stepping into the bed. After all he was going to enjoy this for a complete week and he needed energy for next day.

Evening 4

It was dark when Madhav reached home, as he put on the lights . . . **SURPRISEeeeee** . . . shouted Tanvi, Avani and some more friends of Madhav from Pune. Madhav was taken aback to see all of them . . . Tanvi had arranged for a farewell party for him with help of Avani . . . They played games, songs, masti; leaving them tired in the end . . . Madhav was very happy to meet his friends for 1st time . . . it was the biggest surprise for him he never thought something like this to happen even in his wildest dream. After the party Madhav dropped Tanvi and Avani to their place.

"Tannu . . . This was the best surprise of my life . . . I will never forget this evening . . . Friends mean everything for me . . . you brought them so close to me . . . but I'm still perplexed . . . how did you manage to get all of them . . ."

"Umm . . . that's a secret . . . and suspense . . . that will never be disclosed . . . hehhehe . . . But let me tell you . . . Avani helped me a lot in doing this job . . . she convinced everyone . . ."

"Thanks Avani, and I know even you are not going to reveal the suspense huh right?"

"Exactly . . ." giggled Avani and did a hi five to Tanvi, leaving Madhav wonder how they did this. Girls you know, Madhav tried convincing himself and changed the topic. The trio enjoyed their favorite music and converted the car into a DJ floor.

"It was a pleasure meeting you Avani, thanks to both of you for making this day memorable one . . . I always wanted to thank you personally", said Madhav

Avani looked at him with questioning eyes, "Thank me? For what?"

I know you have a major share in developing my and Tanvi's friendship, I know you got what I mean. I don't need to explain you more. "He winked and Avani shook her head in agreement, "So you mean Im not your friend?" Avani tried to pull his leg . . . "No, not like that . . . in our friendship, Tanvi has a great share and she doesn't even know that . . ." and he gave a sarcastic smile to Tanvi. She was puzzled what they were talking but she showed as if she got everything. After some time they reched home, Madhav waved good bye to them and he drove off as they alighted from the car.

As soon as they reached the flat Tanvi grabbed Avani and started questioning what they both were talking about . . . Avani wanted to try her patience she was not letting the cat out so easily. She was reluctant to tell anything . . . Tanvi finally got upset and started towards her room. When Avani hold her hand and made her sit on the sofa, "Arre buddhu . . . You are such a jerk Tanvi . . . What Madhav meant was, you accepting his friendship and meeting him would have not been possible if I would have opposed. He knows I was never in favor of you talking to him but later after I talked to him I was ok with you two becoming friends and I never resisted after that, If I would have you would have not talked so . . . he was thankful that I did not resist . . ."

"Ohh . . ." exclaimed Tanvi . . . "But why I have share in your and his friendship . . ." Tanvi raised her question innocently.

"You didn't even understand this Tannu . . . OMG! Really? Or you are acting smart huh??"

"No re, now tell me." Tanvi was very curious to know the reason.

"If you would have not talked to him on phone how would I have known him??" Avani questioned raising her eyebrows, expecting Tanvi to now get the obvious answer to her question. "Ok, ok now it's too late we need to sleep now" declared Avani and they both went to sleep

Day 5

Saturday . . . Tanvi loved it so much the most awaited day of the week. Sat was just lovely for the sake that it was a Saturday and it brought with it fun, relaxation, joy and a Sunday to follow. All Saturdays were good but this one was very very special for Tanvi; last day of the week to be with Madhav, then he would be leaving. She wanted this day to be special and so she had planned the day right from early morning, Sinhagad fort was the destination. Tanvi made sure she makes this fun for Madhav early morning they reached the base of the fort; they had planned to trek to the top, so they had started early morning to avoid the sun in late hours. Initially it was good, enthusiastic activity but it was not a childs play, soon Tanvi got tired, they sat for a while on a rock nearby for a while admiring the natural beauty the cool, fresh air was really soothing and soon she was back in spirits, with small small breaks in between finally they reached the top, the fresh air, greenery all around everything made the trek worth. Tanvi was shivering in the cold air, Madhav removed his jacket and gave it to her, and in that oversize jacket Tanvi felt more than comfortable. They took pictures of the fort nature and theirs, once in while Tanvi would give him some more info about the points on the fort. Madhav was impressed by her knowledge, they walked over the fort and the steps; it was refreshing walk. Their skin was glowing in sweat but still felt fresh. After a while they felt hungry, Tanvi took him to one hut and she ordered pair of Pithala Bhakri for them, as they came out to make place for themselves under shade of the tree tanvi noticed Madhav did not like that idea. "Pithala bhakri of this fort is famous all over, you will like it, don't worry."

"No, I'm not worried . . . I'm just concerned about the hygiene." Madhav answered innocently. Tanvi laughed to his answer till it hurt her stomach. After a while she just looked at him and apologizing she said, "You loved the pani puri we had that day besides the road, right? You will love this also . . ."

Madhav nodded and he thought to himself, Tanvi was not like other girls, who would showcase they are so delicate and all. She was rough and tough asal Puneri, though she was not born and brought up in Pune. He admired her for her simplicity and her million dollar smile captured his attention, he could just not move his eyes from her face. In a while their plate of Pithala Bhakari was delivered to them. There was no doubt Madhav would not like it, after all it was Tanvis choice. They ate it and left the place with satisfaction. They roam around the place, It was evening and they thought of spending some time and then leave early so that they can ride back home in time. But God had some different plans . . . as soon as they started descending the fort it started raining heavily, they rushed to get shelter under a tree, it was raining so heavy that the rain drops felt like they were piercing the skin. Tanvi was holding his hand tightly, Madhav was shivering by now. They waited for a while but it was raining heavily and there were no sign that it will stop in a while. Finally they decided to leave.

Running down the slope they caught hold of an auto, shivering they both entered in it and reached home by evening. Madhav dropped her at her place first and then went back to his place. Tanvi called him later in the evening, "How are you feeling?" Tanvi asked him wiping her nose, she had caught cold. Madhav laughed at her guessing her condition and replied, "Girls you know . . . see I was telling you to wear that jacket and I was ok but you were adamant, Im doing all good even without that jacket I can handle, If you would have listened to me you would not be sneezing now . . ." and he again laughed . . .

Tanvi knew she was at fault, so she kept silent, after a while Madhav realized that she was serious and he controlled his laughter and in a serious tone he enquired, "Did you go to the doctor?"

"No . . ." came a plain reply.

"Did you take some medicine?"

"No . . ." Tanvi again replied sniffing her nose.

"Ok dear Im sorry . . . I should not have laughed . . . I will not laugh, now please take some medicine, apply vicks and sleep in your cozy blanket; I hope you are going to come to see off me? You remember na, I'm leaving tomorrow?"

"Yes . . . how did you dare think I will not come to see off . . . Im coming there to help you with packing . . . and you need not worry, I will take medicine and have good sleep so that we can talk tomorrow" Tanvi smiled and Madhav felt better on that reply. Wishing each other Good Night they disconnected the call.

Day 6

It was a Sunday; Tanvi reached his place around 9, She was much better, she helped him all day with his packing. She was with him whole day . . . the day went by as if it never started . . . she accompanied him to the station. They arranged his luggage and sat for a while, they both felt bad. Madhav's train was about to leave, it was time for separation, for next 6 months they won't be able to talk to each other, she was so used to his calls, his voice by now, imagining life without this luxury was difficult.

"I wish I could see the Sea with you", Tanvi sighed in disappointment.

"Hey . . . why don't you come along?" exclaimed Madhav in excitement. "I just have to complete some formalities which won't take much time. I will show you around the place."

The thought was very tempting . . . and while Tanvi gave it a second thought the train started from the station . . . . "But, I don't have ticket . . . I haven't informed anyone . . . Where will I stay???" Tanvi kept asking Madhav . . .

"Relax . . . We will manage . . . came a calm peaceful reply . . ." And Tanvi headed to see Mumbai . . .

"OMG I cannot believe you can do something like this, how can you be so irresponsible . . ." came an angry reply from other side when Tanvi told the situation to Avani. "Anyways now since you have left, there is no use shouting at you. I still cannot believe you did this. Take care. You both enjoy. Mumbai is a cool place, you will like it. Do take care of luggage . . . ohh I forgot . . . you aren't carrying any luggage . . . My aunty is there in Mumbai you could stay at her place. I will inform her that you will be coming . . . take her number 98xxxxxxx . . . be in touch . . . and let me know when you are coming back . . . ." The call got disconnected as there was no range.

"Thank GOD!" sighed Tanvi with a relief . . .

"You are happy the call got disconnected?" Madhav asked confused.

"No I'm happy cause it got disconnected after I took aunt's number from Avani. Avani's aunt stays in Mumbai, she said she will inform her and msg me her address, so I can stay there tonight."

"That's great."

They reached Mumbai around 9 p.m. Madhav took her to aunt's place. After having small conversation, Aunt served them nice supper. After chit chatting for some time Madhav left with a promise to meet next day at 9 a.m. Next day Tanvi got up early, got ready and waited for Madhav. Madhav completed all his formalities and came to pick Tanvi at 10 a.m. Tanvi was a bit disappointed because she had to wait for an hour. But after knowing that he has completed his work . . . she was happy . . . now they can spend time roaming around and site seeing in Mumbai. The day was full of excitement . . . Madhav took her to all his favorite places. They spent a lot of time at the sea shore where Madhav use to be most of the time; it was a serene place, she could not believe her eyes, in a crowded place like Mumbai there could be such a peaceful place. Madhav took her shopping; they went to bandstand . . . saw the new Bandra Worli sea link. From there he also showed her SRK's bungalow . . . Then they went to Mahalaxmi temple, they went to many places, the day seemed to be too small. Finally the moment came when Tanvi had to return back. She gave Madhav the gift which she carried all along with her from Pune.

"Before I open this . . . I too have something for you . . . you have given me the best time I ever had in last few days . . . someone has rightly said . . . The best gift you can give someone, is your Time." saying this he handed the gift to Tanvi.

Tanvi opened it, There was a Happy Man statue smiling back at her . . .

"May GOD give you all the happiness of this world!!! Be happy always as this Happy Man Tannu.

"This is beautiful Maddy, Thanks. Now your turn . . . let me also know if you like my choice."

Madhav opened his gift with lot of excitement, there popped a beautiful "**Fossil**" Watch.

"Tanvi this is too costly, I cannot accept this."

"Maady we won't be meeting for next 6 months now. You are a very special friend, you and Avani are the only two friends in my life. Please don't deny this. I thought a lot as to what I should gift you . . . This watch will always remind you about me every second. That day you said no one is there at home waiting for you . . . but now this watch will keep telling you someone is waiting for you . . ." The train started gaining speed . . . "Keep in touch . . . Bye." Madhav waved bye to Tanvi as he kissed the watch, thanking Tanvi for it.

After Tanvi came home she described all her journey and adventures to Avani, Avani too listened to the minutest detail . . . now Tanvi was not the same girl who left Pune with Madhav. She would always be lost in her thoughts. She would sit hours alone with her Happy Man, as if she was talking to him. She would be in her own world; disconnected from the world. Avani started feeling alone . . . She could not understand Tanvi's behavior . . . She used to be with her all time physically, but she would be wandering somewhere else . . . The only topic they discussed was what Maddy might be doing? When will he return? One day Avani decided to talk to Tanvi . . . She went to Tanvi, who was sitting on a chair looking out of the window nowhere . . .

"Tannu . . . what's going on . . . where are you . . . do you realize . . . I exist? There was a time when this home would come alive when you returned from office. These Days I don't even realize you are sitting next to me. What's the matter? Is everything all right?? You can tell me. We know each other so well. You can talk to me. Tannu are you listening?"

"Hmmm . . . yes I'm . . . is it so?? Have I changed? Why do you feel so? I don't feel like doing anything Avani . . . I'm not able to understand what's going on in my life. My life is out of control . . . Moments from the past keep flashing in front of my eyes. I still feel I'm leaving those last 5 days that I spent with Maddy . . . I'm still in the train, when Maddy come to adieu good bye to me. As the train gains speed I feel I'm leaving back something very important part of my life. I feel emptiness within myself . . . there is a restlessness in me . . . am I going mad?? Am I going insane Avani? Huh? Tell me??"

"Tannu . . . will you listen to me . . . I know you won't agree . . . but if I may . . . I will only say . . . You are in LOVE. I know you might be finding it difficult, you might find it strange and that Tanvi . . . that independent Tanvi is so much dependent on one phone call from Madhav? You are still on the same platform where you left Madhav because you are waiting for the next call from him. For you day starts with his call and ends with his call . . . It might be difficult, as it was your routine since last 6 months . . . but I can tell you . . . this is nothing other than Love. I'm happy for you . . . You have found your soul mate but look at you . . . when Madhav returns if he finds you like this . . . will he like it . . . He would hate himself for what he has done to you . . . won't he? Instead you should prepare for his welcome . . . you should realize you are in Love . . . falling in love is the best thing ever happened to anyone in this world . . . think how will you express to him . . . think about it . . . move ahead in life . . . why do you want to live in past . . . plan your future instead of living in past memories . . . it is good to cherish memories . . . but you should not let them held you back. Take your own time, I'm sure you will realize you are in Love . . .", saying this Avani left the room; leaving Tanvi restless.

Tanvi thought about what Avani said, was that correct? She thought to herself. A couple of days later Tanvi was reading something when she found a

"Only once in your life, you find someone who can completely turn your world around. . . .

. . . .

. . . . Your only hope and security is in knowing that they are a part of your life."

It reflected so much of her heart feelings . . . she was engrossed in reading it and every line brought Madhav's face in front of her and she relived the moment of togetherness they shared, was she in love? Really? She could not believe it. What she was experiencing was LOVE . . . she could not believe it. What should she do? After thinking about this for a long long time . . . After a couple of days . . . she came to conclusion that yes, what Avani was saying was right . . . the discovery was pleasant. After all she had to accept what she was realizing and it was confirmed when she felt exactly what Kajol experienced in the song playing on the Television set, she was experiencing every bit of it in her heart . . .

"Jab kisi ki taraf dil zukne lage . . . baat aake juban par rukne lage, ankhon ankhon mein ikraar hone lage . . . Bol du mein agar tumhe pyaar hone lage . . ."

"I'm in love . . . Ohh My God!!! I can't believe this . . . Madhav . . . is the one . . . the dream boy for whom I waited, whom I saw in my dreams . . . Wow!!!" The discovery was very pleasing. She assured herself and decided to spend time preparing for their future . . . I will cherish our memories . . . I will cherish them . . . how?? Tanvi kept talking to herself . . . After thinking for few days . . . One day Tanvi was very happy as if a million dollar idea has stroked her.

Tanvi went to Avani's room; she was busy cleaning her table. Tanvi went close to her and hugged her from behind, she could no longer control her emotions and she started crying . . . controlling her sobs she could only say . . .

"I'm sorry Avani . . . I have hurt you . . . Actually I didn't know what I was doing . . . I never wanted to hurt your feelings . . . I know how much you value me . . . But I didn't think anything was wrong with me . . . When you pointed out, I really got the seriousness . . . Sorry!!!"

"Hmmm now don't embarrass me . . . I just wanted to make you aware . . . So what have you thought next . . .", consoled Avani.

"Umm I have an idea in mind to surprise him . . . let's . . . see once done I will show it to you"

Tanvi gathered all the pictures of both of them . . . some selective sentimental songs which were close to her heart . . . She combined some selective pictures of all the memorable moments that Madhav and Tanvi shared and created a movie with those selected songs playing in background. Tanvi had put all her heart in making the movie . . . Once that was completed she waited desperately for this 6 months period to end and to meet Madhav.

Chap 7

He Loves Me?

After 6 months . . . It was time for Madhav to come back . . .

I will meet him . . . thought Tanvi to herself . . . what should I say? How should I tell those Magic words to him? Will he also have the same feelings for me? He loves me?? All these questions kept creeping in Tanvi's mind. I hope he takes the initiative . . . with fingers crossed she prayed to GOD. Tanvi kept waiting for Madhav to call . . . but . . . she did not receive his call for many days . . . which only added to her tension . . . After waiting for a week she decided to call him . . . She called him, his cell started ringing . . . With every ring her heart beat increased . . . with every ring that was not answered, questions started building in her mind . . . is he avoiding me? May be he doesn't want to talk to me . . . .

After 2-3 calls Madhav answered her call

"Hey . . . Tannnu . . . hi, how are you . . . what's up? I thought you forgot I'm back in the city . . . hehehe . . ." giggled Madhav.

"I'm doing good . . . Is it? If you were waiting for my call why didn't you pick my call? And I thought you would call me to inform you are back?"

"Ohhh . . . I was taking bath when you called . . . I was about to call you after seeing your missed calls . . . hmmm Sorry to disappoint you . . . Actually I wanted to meet you . . . I need to tell you a very important decision I have taken about my future . . . so can we meet tomorrow?"

"Ya sure . . . I would love to see you . . . ok then see you tomorrow . . ." saying this Tanvi disconnected the call, with lots of expectations built up in her mind.

Next day . . . both Tanvi and Madhav were excited to meet each other. They prepared for the evening from the morning, what they wanted to tell each other . . . Madhav practiced his sentences . . . nth time. Tanvi also tried to prepare herself . . . finally the moment came when they were going to be face to face. Tanvi was wearing a sea green color embroidered silk salwar suit, with matching earrings; her hairs were loosely tied, and a string of hair was falling on her face. She was playing with the pendant in her chain that complemented her dress; she kept observing the surroundings, the ambience around as she waited for Madhav. The place was perfect . . . a fountain added its own unique strikes to the light music playing in the background . . . soft breeze flowing kept swinging Tanvi's string of hair and Tanvi kept tugging it to her ear. Every sec that passed was increasing the apprehension of the meet. The questions that needed to be answered, the curiosity of her first proposal, will he accept? Every sec was passing like a year. Madhav came there at right time, he knew she hates late comers, he was wearing a blue jeans and a light orange color T-Shirt, his military cut, with sparkle in this eyes and killing smile added to his valorous look. But his nervousness could not escape Tanvi's notice.

"Hi Tannu . . . I hope you didn't have to wait long . . ." said Madhav as he gave Tanvi a beautiful bouquet of red roses.

"Thank you, they are beautiful, even I came just 5 min back." smiled back Tanvi . . . "So what is it . . . you said you wanted to meet me . . ." enquired Tanvi . . . "Trying to be innocent, behaving as if she didn't know why he wanted to meet . . . and even she was desperately waiting for this moment . . ."

"Ummm . . . yes . . . actually these 6 months . . . I was thinking about only one thing . . . you know what . . . about **you . . .** I only longed for one thing . . . to hear your voice . . . I wanted to do only one thing . . . call you . . . I had been so keen to come back and call you . . . hear your voice . . . but somehow . . . When I came back I could not gather the courage to call you and tell I'm back . . . I just could not understand my behavior . . . I . . . "

Madhav kept struggling with words . . . and Tanvi kept looking into his eyes . . . she thought to herself, encouraged him to say what she wanted to hear, but everything was happening in her mind she talked to her heart where he and only he resided, I know what you want to say she said to herself . . . but I want to hear it from you Maddy . . . just say it once . . . and say it in a way that this moment becomes memorable for lifetime . . . Tanvi thought to herself. He signaled to a waiter; in a blink before Tanvi could understand anything Madhav was on his knees, in the background "If I had to live my life without you need me . . . the days would all be empty . . . I don't want to live without you . . . Nothing's gonna change my love for you . . ." was playing softly but distinct enough to set the mood. Madhav on his knees took Tanvi's hand in his hand kissed it and adding all his heart to the words said,

Jaise roshni insaan ko raah dikhati hai,
Phool muskurahat dete hai,
Saanse zindagi deti hai,
Dhadkan life deti hai,
Wiase hi tumahara saath muzhe zindagi jine ki prerna deta hai,
Aaj mein jina sikhata hai,

Mera Dil, Kisiko apnese zyda apna bananeki khwayish karta hai,

So can you be mine, my better half for the life-time!!!

I love you dear very much, which can't be put in words, you can only feel it.

When you are with me the world seems to be with me, but when you are not with me there is nothing in my life.

Wo Paas rahe ya dur, Nazron main samaye rehte hai koi hume itna bata de kya isi ko muhabaat kehte hai?
Kya tumhe bhi muzhse pyaar hia?
"Kaho na pyaar hai! . . ."

Tanvi was on cloud 9 . . . she was so happy . . . He loves me . . . he loves me . . . she said to herself . . . her heart was jumping with joy, collecting herself together trying to reply and hiding her mixed feelings she could only say,

My day starts with your voice & ends when I say Good Night to you, now a days, I spend my time only thinking about you! When I come in front of you something happens within me . . . which I have never experienced before!!!

Meri saanse tham jaati hai aur dhadkane bhad jaati hai Is ehasaas main, mann hamesha khush rahata hai

Wafadari ki woh rasmain
Nibhayenge hum woh kasmain
Tum kabhi na chodna mera haath
Haan muzhe bhi tumhse pyaar hai!!!

Madhav felt as if all his tension and sleepless nights that he spent were worth this moment. he was too happy.They both looked at each other . . . they had so much to tell each other but nothing was being expressed, their lips were silent, only eyes spoke. After a long pause, Madhav said, "Today is the happiest day of my life . . . I won't forget these moments for my lifetime . . . I just can't imagine my life if your response would have been otherwise."

Madhav took out a ring and blinked at her, she gave him her hand, slowly the ring drifted in her finger, before Tanvi could appreciate the ring, and she was already on the dance floor with Madhav.

"Tu ru tu ru . . . tu ru tu . . . para ri ra ra . . . pyaar Toh Hona hi tha . . . ." Remo started singing for them setting the stage on fire for them . . .

They danced till they were panting. The evening went splendid; both enjoyed a lot making it their memorable one. Madhav went to drop Tanvi.

Tanvi was in a new state, she loved everything that was happening in her life. At touch of love everyone becomes a poet, they say. Everything feels good. Tanvi thought of writing down all her experiences. She wanted to capture these moments forever so that when she reads them she experiences the moments, lives those moments again . . . Every day after she came back home she would sit down close her eyes and relive the moments spent with Madhav, then jot down them as she had experienced them word by word . . . moment by moment. That day she came tired, though it was a tiring journey the joy the day had brought could not escape being noted in her diary. With tired hands she opened her diary and started turning pages, she closed her eyes and started recollecting the whole day and as it started appearing before her eyes she started making note of it . . . .

"Nilkanteshwar and that is final!" declared Maddy. We were deciding to visit some picnic spot for the weekend and were not able to conclude. Maddy had already visited the place, he loved the place and he wanted me to visit it too. I did not want to go to a temple. That would off course, be last on the list of a new couple planning for an outing. But who would argue with Maddy so finally we were heading to

Nilkanteshwar. It was about 2 hour journey. The ride at back of the bike was very pleasing; we started early morning so that we can reach before the Sun starts heating. The cool breeze felt soothing. Enjoying the early morning beauty we didn't realize we had even reached the base of temple, which was a hill from there we had to trek to the top.

Wow!! I was so excited, though I thought this was going to be a boring trip it had its own share of adventure. We had to nearly trek for 4 km from base to reach the top, the hill was very steep which needed lot of effort to move forward at every step and soon I was gasping for air, while Maddy looked ok. He looked back and checking my tired eyes he said "Ohh, my darling is finding this difffficult? Who was saying this is going to be boring huh?" I just gave him a not interested look and continued my trek. He teased me a lot for being weak. I realize it now, because of his teasing I climbed with more energy, a feeling inside me told me, no I'm not weak I can do this and I would start with a new zeal. I took many small breaks on my way, some for water some for oxygen; I had never experienced so much exhaustion in my life. I cursed Maddy a lot, it was all because of him instead of enjoying the trip I was completely exhausted. Finally the moment arrived when we reached the temple; the first glimpse that my tired eyes covered with sweat had was marvelous, a huge Shiva statue stood in front of me to welcome me in middle of a pond . . . The statue was so wonderful and beautiful that admiring the beauty I did not apprehend when my tiredness vanished. Maddy was so excited to show me round the place. There were so many statues and every statue had a story to tell. We clicked pictured with some; I was trying to create memories. It was no way just a temple. We had lot of fun, I gained historical knowledge about the place and the characters and also learnt something about Maddy, he remembered me believing in Shiva and so he was keen on showing me the temple, He drove for 2 hours just for me to let me witness sanctity of the place. It was a calm, peaceful place where all your worries would find a solution. God is really great, at his feet, I forgot the pain coming there had caused. The birds chirping around, that sound had lost in the sound of machines in the city. The breeze flowing there was pure. Every corner was telling a story of valor. I could not believe there was such a serene place in Pune.

Then Maddy took me to a point from where Khadakwasla dam was visible, backwaters of panshet, the view was scenic. I loved the time we spent together there. While descending I had no trouble; running down through the steep slope was fun, especially when Maddy was worried about my safety and shouting after me to watch my way. In short I had lot of fun, it was a memorable trip!!

As she finished reading it she could not resist the temptation of reading it and experiencing the trip again . . . she read it aloud to herself happy about her achievement.

Tanvi and Madhav spent all these days (6 months to measure) with each other, Tanvi collected all these beautiful jwels and collected them in her diary, they were going to help her live for the next 6 months as it was time for Madhav to leave . . . They both had gathered a lot of memories that would help them catch up with this separation time . . . this time Madhav promised Tanvi that he would be back in 3 months . . . and he would permanently come back he would leave this job and look for a new one in Pune itself, making their life easy . . . which provided some comfort to Tanvi; It was time for him to leave . . . They were at the station looking into each other wishing that the time goes still, spending every sec with each other suddenly Tanvi realized she missed something she took out a packet from her purse and gave it to Madhav.

"I made this long back and wanted to gift it to you as a welcome gift but somehow forgot . . . So anyways . . . accept it as a farewell gift . . . And I have updated this to add all the moments we spent in these 6 months together" Tanvi said, handing the packet which had the CD, which contained the movie she had prepared about the two of them . . . "This will always remind you how our relation began and I wish it will always be as fresh as it is in this CD."

"Thanks Tanvi . . . but . . . I could not get anything for you but . . ."

"Your promise to come back soon and hope to see you settled in Pune are my best ever gift . . . try to come early . . . I won't need any other gift." smiled back Tanvi.

"Yes. I will try. Believe me these are the best days of my life, I will try my best to come back in 3 months . . . take good care of my heart . . . I'm leaving my '**Amanat**' with you . . . don't hurt her. "said Madhav turning to Avani.

"Yes boss . . ." grinned back Avani. Just then the train moved . . . They waved Good-Bye.

Initial few days were very troublesome for Tanvi, each night she would look in the sky searching for the special pair of stars that she and Madhav had named after each other she wished they could also be together always as these starts . . . but the star made her realize he is very close to her than it looks under the same sky, somewhere he is, he might also be observing the same stars!!! Somehow he will come to know how much she misses him. Every sec that passed brought a new hope in her that the time to meet is now coming closer; needless to say she spent many sleepless nights . . .

One day Tanvi was waiting for Riya at CCD, when she looked at the CCD logo "A Lot can happen over Coffee" After reading it she went in her thoughts . . . It was so true . . . if she would have not met Madhav that day . . . her life would have been different, would she have been in love, this whole episode of her life would have not happened. She shook her head in agreement . . . just then Riya came . . . there were lot of tensions going on at work that time and Tanvi was very tensed . . . She felt she could not handle the situation. Riya was senior to her but a good friend of hers and was in Pune for a short term business requirement she was going to leave that day and so they had decided to meet at CCD where they could share their feelings . . . Tanvi could also get to hear secrets of newly wedded life of Riya, after talking to her Tanvi felt much relaxed . . .

After chatting for some time and having coffee they left; Riya had to leave for Mysore, so was in a hurry. As they were coming down from the stairs Tanvi slipped and felled down, she was unconscious. This tensed Riya, she took her to hospital; Riya had to rush to station and Tanvi was unconscious, not knowing what she should do she called up Avani who reached there soon, Avani thanked Riya and asked her to leave as she had to catch her train for Mysore; Riya left instructing Avani to call her in case of any issues. As Riya left, the doctor came there. Avani was very nervous, as the doctor came she enquired about Tanvi, "She is ok now. There is small injury on her head. But it's not that serious. She will get well soon. What is your relation with the patient?"

"I'm Avani, her friend Ma'am, her roommate, we stay together in Kalyaninagar."

"There is nothing serious but I would like to talk to her family members can they come here."

"Ma'am we have been together since 8 years, we are like sisters you can tell me. Her parents stay in Kerala. If it's something serious I will call them but why to trouble them if I can manage it. Is it money? Do we need to do some operation? You tell me Ma'am if it needs them to be here I will surely call them."

Ok come to my cabin. As they both had their seat in the doctor's cabin the doc started, "Look Avani, I think you should call her parents, there is one problem as I see . . . Your friend Tanvi is pregnant."

"What??? What are you saying Doc?" replied Avani in shock.

Chap 8
Love Blossoms

Avani was very disturbed by the doctor's reply; she didn't know what to do. How could Tanuu do such a mistake? Avani kept thinking; she felt her mind going blank. She was sitting next to Tanvi in the hospital room, Tanvi was still unconscious. Avani felt restless . . . as she kept looking down towards the floor blankly, Tanvi came to consciousness, digesting her restlessness, and Avani took Tanvi's hand in her hand . . .

"How are you feeling now Tannu are you ok??" She called the doctor. After routine checkup Tanvi was discharged from hospital. Avani took her to home . . . till this time Avani had controlled all her temper and anxiety. Once they reached home, Avani could not suppress her feelings any more . . .

"Tannu how are you feeling now?" Avani asked Tanvi with lot of more questions to follow in her eyes which Tanvi read her eyes.

"I know Avani what you want to ask . . . I can understand your condition . . . Doctor told me . . . I know I'm 3 months pregnant . . . don't look surprise . . ."

"So now what? How could you do this Tannu?? What will your parents go through when they will come to know this? Did you think about them for once before doing such shameful act?"

Tanvi kept mum . . . she had no idea what to say how to reply . . . She was scared . . . she could not face Avani . . . how will she face her parents?? All these questions kept troubling her . . .

"Avani, I know you won't agree to this . . . but will you listen to me for a sec . . . see . . . Maddy will be coming next month, I will talk to my parents about him then and then I will even tell them about all this . . . but till then please can we keep this a secret . . . I promise you, I will tell my parents the day he comes back . . ."

"What if Madhav is not ready to take responsibility of this child? Do you realize Tannu you have put yourself into such a difficult situation . . . not only you . . . me, your parents, everyone who loves you . . . even Maddy . . ."

"But Avani this is not whole and soul my fault . . . It all happened . . . I mean . . . There is never a time or place for true love. It happens accidentally, in a heartbeat, in a single flashing, throbbing moment. I did not realize . . . how I can tell you . . . How can you say I have put him in trouble? Isn't this even his responsibility?"

"Yes . . . it is . . . but I think you should have acted more responsibly . . . How can you be little you parents expectations, their faith in you? How can you be sure Madhav will accept this situation?"

"Believe me Avani . . . I have loved him . . . He is a responsible person . . . It's just a matter of few days, He had promised me he will come back as soon as possible . . . he said he will be coming back in 3 months . . . he will be leaving this job and will try for a new one in Pune . . . everything will be all right . . . please don't take tension . . . can you keep this secret for a few days for me . . ."

"Uhhhhhhh . . . Sighed Avani . . . well what can I say . . . It's your life . . . whatever you want from me . . . just give it a thought . . . and have rest now" saying so Avani left the room

Tanvi just hoped Madhav would come back soon and help her out of this situation. Silently she prayed to GOD . . . From her bed side window she looked at the sky . . . and found her special pair of stars . . . Looking at them she said . . . "Maddy . . . I'm waiting for you . . . come soon . . ." The clouds in the sky took her back in her memories . . .

It was a cloudy evening . . . same clouds had gripped the sky, Madhav and Tanvi had been to a movie to Esquare, by the time the movie came to an end it was raining cats and dogs outside. Madhav insisted to wait till it stops raining . . . but Tanvi wanted to enjoy the rain on bike while on ride . . . so she insisted that they should leave . . . Madhav could not argue . . . They both enjoyed the rain for some time but driving was getting difficult for Madhav as it was raining too heavy . . . so finally they decided to stop at Madhav's place which was nearby. It was late night, Tanvi wanted to go home and rain was not ready to stop. Both of them were swamped in water, they sat at the steps leading to garden, watching the rain and hoping it will stop soon . . . They kept chatting, Tanvi told Madhav about her family.

"My dad cares for me a lot, he is very strict though and I have got many bashings from him in childhood but I still love him a lot, he is my role model . . . Mom too . . . she is a darling . . . very sweet she always protects me from getting bashings . . ." chuckeled Tanvi . . . "From childhood I have been always listening to my parents like an obedient child . . . School friends . . . ? There are not many to list . . . hehehe . . . The whole class was my friend. I was always target of my teachers because I played very elvish tricks but at the same time they all loved me a lot. I got the best student award. But now life has changed . . . I hardly get time to participate in any extracurricular activity . . . You know Maddy . . . sometimes I think was it me who got all those awards . . . who was so active all the time? Now?? Look at me . . . I sit in front of that computer in office and in front of the idiot box at home."

"Hmmm . . . sounds interesting . . ." agreed Madhav rubbing his hands to get some warmth.

The lamp in the garden added beautiful color to the rain drops falling in the spectrum of its light. They both watched it and suddenly Tanvi ran towards the lamp trying to catch the rain drops . . . Madhav ran behind her . . . trying to bring her back but Tanvi would not listen . . . she kept running and Madhav kept chasing her and persuading her to get back inside . . . finally he got hold of her, both were gasping and they sat down to breathe for a while . . . Madhav got up and ran inside he put on music and came back running, gasping he asked Tanvi for a dance . . . the atmosphere was cool and perfect for a rain dance, Tanvi gave him her hand and with his support got up . . .

"Yeh jo sajish hai boondoin ki . . . dekho na . . . dekhno na . . . Hawa jo hole hole . . . san sanan san . . ." started playing in the background and they both lost in each other's eyes started slowly moving their bodies, after dancing to their heart's content and enjoying to fullest they came back in the living room. Both were drenched in water and shivering. Madhav went in and brought his kurta pyjama for Tanvi, which he thought could fit her . . . it was still cold outside.They both changed and got comfortable . . . Tanvi dried Madhav's hair for him. She dried her hair for a while but being long they were going to take time, she thought of using a dryer but dropped the idea as there was no electricity. While she rubbed her hair with towel Madhav called out,

"Tannu it seems we will have to eat bread butter and fruits for dinner . . ." as he scanned his fridge

"It's ok . . . anyways I'm not hungry. Taste of the burger we had is still lingering in my mouth."

Madhav brought some fruits and bread packet, they sat on the dining table to have their dinner, and as he started to serve the lights went off, Madhav went and fiddling around brought candle, he lit it and placed it on the table, as he was getting back to his seat he looked at Tanvi, in that dim candle light she looked nothing less than an Angel, her wet curly hair some falling on her face, added to her natural beauty, as he scanned her thoroughly he stopped at her hands which were playing with her chain pendant, around her neck. Soft breeze that was flowing would give him a broader view of her neckline once in a while. He could not resist but admire her, something disturbed him, and made him think, confused, he was trying to make sure what he was thinking was correct, he thought to himself, "We were completely sodden by water, I'm sure she is not wearing it." He gave himself a logical reasoning and tried to answer his questions himself. After getting that answer, he could not help but look at them, rather he stared at them. Tanvi took the bread and as she ate he could see them prominently when they got pressed by her arms and Madhav kept staring at them, Tanvi caught him starting at one such moment and mischievously said, "You are staring as if you have never seen one." On that Madhav gulped and nodded to say no innocently.

"Really?" the tone turned mischievous. He again nodded and blushed on getting caught and scolded himself for his act.

"Ohh . . . so that is the reason I see, I now know why you gave me this kurta, It has no buttons huh? . . . umm?" Tanvi said sarcastically pulling the two ends of her kurta apart to show that it didn't have buttons . . . feeling offended Madhav . . . immediately replied "no, no . . . not like that . . ."

"I know your intentions now, you mawali . . ." Tanvi got up and went closer to him.

"Tannu . . . I'm a decent guy . . . I had no intentions like that . . ." Madhav said putting the knife apart, with help of which Tanvi had lifted his face . . . "Let's butter the bread . . ." and he took the knife from her, took a bread and started applying butter to it. After a while he raised his eyes to see what Tanvi was doing, she was standing there silently and looked a bit disappointed.

"Here . . . have this you will like it" Madhav said giving her a quarter orange that he had started peeling to her.

"I don't believe you are a decent guy any more" Madhav was shocked by that statement, "Tannu . . . you have been with me for so many days, did you ever feel I desire for you physically, dear . . . it just happened . . . just because I stared . . . that too it happened that I looked at you when the wind blew the ends apart, What do you expect this kaniz to do? if the atmosphere turns so romantic, the candle lights and rain add to it and to top it your half dried hair are making the kurta wet, revealing the hidden treasures, the more I try to concentrate on my work the aroma that your wet body has spread, uff . . . Tannu please notice that after all I'm a Guy . . . I will go crazy if you know it comes in view effortlessly, right? I did not mean to hurt you by staring . . ."

"shh . . . ok . . . Let's have a test of you decency . . . If you pass I will believe you." Tanvi didn't let him complete his sentence.

"Ok . . . I have no problem . . . I can prove to you I'm a decent guy . . ."

"What if I prove that you are a mawali? Like those loafer types?" Then there was silence for a while Tanvi continued, "Ok whoever wins the other person has to do whatever he wishes? Deal?" Tanvi said moving ahead her hand,

"Deal" Madhav confirmed placing his hand on hers.

"Ok . . . so get me the buttons of this Kurta first . . ." Tanvi said.

"Ok . . . how many are there, you see the buttons of this Kurta are different, they are tied up with a string together and they are delicate so I remove them otherwise they can get damaged when I wash them I will . . ." Tanvi cut him in between and said . . . "I don't know how many are there you count them yourself . . ." and she stood there in front of him, Madhav started counting them from top to bottom, as his eyes moved down, he could not escape noticing the curves, "One . . . twwwooo, thrr . . . three . . . F . . .ff" he started stammering and his voice was breaking . . . "My lallu . . . doesn't even know his numbers . . . you are so weak in math hmm?" Tanvi teased him knowing his condition "See . . . we are yet to start the test and you have failed . . ."

Madhav went in and brought the buttons and placed them in front of her in his hand. Tanvi gave him what should I do with them kind of look and said "What? Tug them now for me? Let's see if you can do that"

"What?? That's it . . . off course I can . . ." He said and came closer to her, they were facing each other and Tanvi stood there with her hands folded back, which gave Madhav a signal that she is not going to help but make it more difficult as that made the kurta expose more of her skin. Madhav started tugging the buttons, the first couple was easy, he enjoyed it while his hand brushed against her skin, she felt so soft just like silk, after that started the real test, as he moved down he stopped, his hands started shivering, he was not able to concentrate, the firm round shape, was so much inviting he had a deep urge within to feel them but he reminded himself . . . you are a decent guy . . . decent guy . . . He pulled the kurta and tried putting the button, he could feel the depth down there, the ups and downs . . . He was confirmed by now, she was not wearing it. The dim light, soft breeze, her body scent everything added and the situation was very erotic for Madhav the silence between the two made him think, what she might be thinking about him at this moment. Just then the electricity came and music started playing in background

"Oouch!! Dhak dhak karne laga . . . mara jiya ra darne laga . . . sayain bayein mode na . . . kacchi kaliyan tod na . . ."

Ohh God . . . Madhav thought for a while . . . and cursed himself for not putting the CD player off before accepting this challenge every other electric item was off only the CD player was left on. He controlled his emotions as far as he could. The touch of her skin was so erotic . . . He looked at Tanvi, she was standing still, eyes closed, and he continued in the dim candle light fiddling with the buttons, finally Tanvi broke the silence . . . "So you have never seen one before huh?" Madhav just nodded helping his hand concentrate and complete the task . . . "How are you feeling Maddy?" Tanvi asked naughtily. "What answer do you want?" "Only the truth. I want to know what thoughts are going across your mind, what is your heart feeling" She declared.

"I'm witnessing Gods ultimate creation . . . what do you think I might be feeling like? It feels like I'm out of this world Tannu right now . . ."

"Wanna see one of those creations?" Madhav looked at her trying to check if he heard her correct . . . ". . . wanna feel it?" before he could come out of her naughty eyes, Tanvi took his hand and slid it inside the kurta and he was feeling them, witnessing the softness . . . they were so wonderful, not too small not too big . . . perfect enough to fill his palms completely "It feels like heaven . . . Tannu . . ." he uttered after a while. He moved the kurta a bit to the left, being oversized for her he could see her bare shoulder, he kissed her through her neckline slowly, then her shoulder, then very slowly back to her neck up to the jaw through the jaw line to her ear, and kissing her earlobe he softly whispered "*I love you . . .*", sending shivers through every inch of her, removing his hand he tugged the last couple of buttons and went back to the table . . . He was silent; maybe he did not like losing the challenge. "So you proved you are a decent guy huh?" Madhav looked at her bewildered while she continued, "off course you are Maddy . . . you think I have a doubt regarding that? It was me who could not control the feeling that your touch brought . . . I wanted to feel you down there . . . I watched you for the whole time, those deep blue eyes, I know you controlled your desires and you were in full control of yours. I wanted to feel your touch. Everything has a value only if someone is there to value it, you see . . . without you I have no value. I'm all yours Maddy, you can do anything with me without feeling guilty about it, I will be yours forever and ever, and I cannot see your eyes filled with guilt . . . ok??" she smiled and came closer to him and she moved her hand through his hair and bent down, kissing his ear she whispered . . . "I love you too and will love you till eternity" Madhav smiled back and kissed her hand and made her sit beside him. "hmm so you are all mine?" Madhav repeated her sentence to confirm, "Yes . . ." assured Tanvi . . . "You are my property?" "Yes dear . . . you have any doubt . . ." "My Private property . . ." Madhav said getting up and hugged her from behind the chair "Let me put my seal then . . ." he said mischievously coming closer to her, Tanvi crinkle at first but then let it go his way, she stood there sturdy expecting act from him, not disappointing her he kissed her on her forehead then her eyes followed by nose, he stopped at her lips, Tanvi was tranquil; feeling his breath on her face, eyes closed in anticipation of his next move. After spending a while in his thought weather to go or not he moved his finger across her lips slowly, Tanvi opened her eyes, he kissed his finger and winked at her throwing a kiss to her with his eyes and went back to his chair. Tanvi blushed and kept smiling to herself, feeling the his touch that was still lingering on her skin. Madhav kept on looking at her; he was getting to see this shy, stealing glances kind of Tanvi for the first time. Otherwise she would always carry the bold and beautiful look. Even though the electricity was back, they did not put on the lights, Madhav felt it pleasant to see her face glow in the candlelight, water drizzling out of her wet hair. They were lost in their world.

They had some fruits, bread butter whatever and had the most romantic dinner of their life; with love they fed each other. "It seems rain won't stop . . . do one thing stay at my place today . . ." Madhav said looking worried.

"Huh?? What are you saying Maddy . . . I have office tomorrow . . ." said Tanvi playfully.

"I will drop you early morning . . . to your place, and Madam don't forget I won the challenge, you have to listen to me huh?" Madhav winked.

"Ummhmm. Hmm I have to . . . ok, I'm already feeling sleepy. Where am I sleeping?" Madhav showed her the room and went to get blanket for her. When Madhav came back Tanvi was preparing her bed, water droplets were falling from her half dried hair, and her hair covered her face. Madhav went by her side and hugged her . . . Tanvi turned to him which made her hair fall on her face covering her eyes . . . Madhav kept looking at her half covered face; Tanvi was firm in his arms, not knowing how to react. Madhav pulled her towards him, their bodies pressed against each other. Tanvi could hear his heart beat; with utmost care he moved her hair from her face, and eyes which were too shy to make contact with his . . . for a moment the air went still, they both were still . . . Madhav gave Tanvi a passionate kiss on her forehead and let her go . . . Tanvi tightly hugged him back, "Don't leave me", breaking the silence, said Tanvi resting her head on Madhav's chest; She loved the feeling of being cared by him, resting her head on his chest listening his heart beat for her. Madhav obeyed the order.

"Hold me now, touch me . . . I don't wanna live without you . . ." played in background softly.

They stayed there in each other arms for a while. The air started gaining heat . . . Madhav pushed back Tanvi's hair from her shoulder, and kissed her neck. The warmth of his lips left Tanvi with a sigh. Tanvi loosened the half-hoop of diamonds on her left hand and held it out to him playfully and ran across the room, while he chased at a point she lost her control and had to surrender to Madhav, finally the moment came when she was in his arms bewildered, appreciating her beauty Madhav bent towards her and they had their first lip kiss . . . Tanvi was lost in him, half dead in shyness, she was swift off the floor by Madhav in his arms and he led her to the bed where their souls unite.

"Tannuu . . . where are you I'm calling you for dinner since such a long time come . . . let's have dinner . . . there's no electricity . . . seems we will have to do without it tonight . . ." called out Avani, bringing Tanvi back to present.

"Umm I'm not hungry Avani, you carry on . . ."

"Tannuu . . . did I hurt you? I think I did . . . I shouldn't have been harsh to you . . . I'm sorry. I'm with you so don't worry . . . everything will be ok. Madhav will come soon."

"Thanks Avi . . . I knew you will understand."

"Will uncle aunty agree to your marriage . . . is caste and all a problem . . ."

"Huh?? We never talked about such matter at home . . . but I'm sure they will, Maddy is such a good guy he will win their hearts. Caste and alll? Ummm can be a problem . . . but even Maddy doesn't know his caste . . . so what's the big deal, we can tell he is of same caste . . ." blinked Tanvi as if a million dollar idea stroked her.

"Ummhmmm . . . ya that can be done . . . Don't worry Tanuu . . . I will help you convince them I will praise Madhav in front of them . . . tell them how you both make a good couple . . . I hope that will be enough . . . He is a settled person good looking, polite what else will parents look for in a guy for their daughter? I'm confident they will agree to your marriage. Meanwhile you can prepare them day by day . . . so that this does not come to them as a shock."

"Ahhh, yes that is a good idea but I want him to come first."

"Ok . . . anyways . . . When is he returning . . ."

"I guess he should be here in a week's time." Tanvi said chewing her food.

"Good . . . ok . . . Now I hope you are hungry . . . huh??" asked Avani rolling her eyes.

"Yes . . . I'm . . ." chuckled Tanvi.

After having dinner, Tanvi returned back to her room while she kept looking at her star, she fell asleep. After waiting for 15 days Tanvi tried Madhav's cell but in vain. "Do you have his mail Id? May be his work is extended . . . you can ask him to come for some days sort out this matter and he can return."

"No Avani I don't have his mail Id. We never thought we would need that. I don't even know which country he has gone. I have no other way to contact him. I have no other option rather than waiting for him . . ."

Tanvi kept calling him each day n number of times . . . in a hope that she will get in touch with him as soon as he is back in Pune. Time was ticking on and tension prevailed. Avani was a great support for her. She took great care of her food, health and kept her promise that she did to Madhav. She also wanted him to come back soon . . . "Madhav I want you to come back and take care of your Amanat . . . We don't have enough time . . . there's a lot to do after you come . . . I don't know how you are going to take all this. We are going ahead with lot of assumptions" she thought to herself, the thought scared her . . . neglecting the negative thought coming to her mind . . . Everything's going to be fine . . . Think good think good . . . she told herself.

Chap 9

THE UGLY TRUTH

Time and tide waits for none. It had been 5 months, Madhav did not come back. Tanvi and Avani were very worried.

"Tannu . . . I know this will hurt you but . . . I don't think he is coming back. May be he was also like the rest; he was not what he showcased you he was. In my opinion he will not come, if he wanted to be back and due to any emergency he could not he would have contacted you . . . he knows you are waiting . . . Why did he promise to be back in 3 months?"

Tanvi could no longer hold back her tears . . . as if Avani talked about her greatest fear . . . she cried uncontrollably . . . .

"Tannu . . . it's not easy for me . . . but we don't have any other option . . . You abort the child . . ."

"What?? No . . . no . . . Avi . . . is this you . . . no . . . may be he didn't love me, and all he did to me was a fraud . . . but what about me . . . I loved him . . . I still love him . . . and I still have hope that he will return . . . May be these days that I spent with him was with an image that was not of his . . . but I have loved this image . . . and I cannot kill my love . . . I'm sorry but I cannot do this . . . Don't ask me to do this . . . Please Avani Please . . ." pleaded Tanvi.

"Tannuu . . . Do you know what you are saying . . . what are you going to tell your parents? Delivering a baby is not that easy . . . do you know what you are saying? Think practically . . . What you will have to go through afterwards?"

"Hmm . . . I know it's not easy . . . yes . . . but I'm ready to face it . . ."

"Why do you want to punish the innocent child . . . It's none of his mistake . . . Don't think emotionally . . . think practically . . ."

"Punish him??? Am I? How can I Avani?"

"What are you talking Tannu . . . Can't you see . . . Have you thought what all things he will have to face in this world . . . he will have to listen to the worlds taunts . . . And how are you going to manage without your family support?? No one's parent will agree to this suicide . . . listen to me . . . we still have this option open . . . Are you listening to me??"

"Avani . . . let's not talk about this . . . I'm firm on my decision whatever happens I'm going to deliver this baby", saying this Tanvi left the room . . . and went to her room; she shut the door loud, started the radio on high volume . . . and sat on the bed with a thud trying to control her emotions from flowing through her eyes.

"Nahin samne ye alag baat hai . . . mere saath hai tu . . . mere saath hai . . ." Played in the background igniting the anger in her . . . thinking about her conversation with Avani, hating herself for nth time.

She took her diary and got lost in his memories, as she surfed through the pages all moments of togetherness started running in front of her eyes as if she watched a movie. She stopped at one page, she closed her eyes took a deep sigh and she started reading it . . . .

Our plan for today included visit to water kingdom, since Maddy wanted me to be with him and he had some work in Mumbai we went to Mumbai, he wanted to take me to water kingdom, even he had not visited the place, it did not fascinate me much since I loved natural things, still since it was a new place for him we thought of enjoying the rides there, Water being our weakness and common love; we did a thorough search of rides a week before, we were very excited, we had been planning for this trip since a week. We didn't want to miss a sec of the fun so had started early morning to avoid traffic and reach there by 8 am. When we reached there we felt like we were the first couple to reach there and the gate keeper is going to tell us, we need to wait it's still not time for the park to open. With hesitation we started towards the gate, as expected the keeper stopped us and enriched us with disheartening information—the park was closed for renovation from yesterday till next month. What??? Was the expression we both carried on our face. Ohh noo . . . The whole mood was spoiled; we were so excited to take the rides. Maddy too was sad. With lost hopes we started moving to the bike, as we started the return journey Maddy took an unexpected turn, I enquired him where we were heading? To which he answered he didn't knew . . . we were driving like crazy not knowing the destination, I loved the ride, especially because we were driving out of Mumbai and the air was clean, soothing. I don't know where we were heading and I was least bothered, with Maddy besides me I had no fear. I enjoyed the ride, after a while we touched the highway he increased the speed . . . I loved it, wind blowing on the face, hushing in my ears; I could not see anything in front, just had to feel!! Wow . . . I exclaimed and hugged him. But suddenly the pleasure turned into fear . . . he was driving crazy . . . The speedometer showed max speed . . . I was scared now . . . .

"Slow down. This is scaring me." I cried in horror . . . he was not able to hear me because of the speeding wind . . . I repeated myself 3-4 times . . . then he responded . . .

"Scaring you?? Are you all right . . . isn't this fun. You love this . . ." he just winked at me.

"No I don't, it's not fun. Please, slow down . . . it's too scary!"

He thought for a while, this was a good time for revenge he thought to keep me scared for some more while, he rode the bike now in zig zag manner . . .

By now I was half dead, "Stop it . . . you are scaring me . . . !!" I shouted . . . or I pleaded . . . right pleaded is the right word.

"Then tell me, do you love me??" He asked decreasing the speed a little . . .

"Off course I do . . . why on earth I would come on a death ride with you otherwise . . ."

"Will you love me for whole life?" He questioned me.

"Yes my dear . . ." Was my obvious answer "and I want to spend whole of my life besides you . . . but not in hospital . . . dear please slow down . . ."

"Ok I will but if I get a hug and a sweet kiss . . ." he demanded, he was getting notorious

"What . . . ?? are you crazy . . . slow down first . . . then u will get whatever you ask for . . . ."

"No . . . My kiss first . . ." he was reluctant

"OMG . . . please . . . slow down . . ." but he didn't listen to anything, no argument was reaching his ears . . . was he doing all that on purpose I don't know but I was scared to death and so I kissed him.

"And my hug??" His demands were increasing I was already holding him tight . . .

I pleaded, "Can't you feel it, I'm already hugging you please . . . for God's sake slow down . . . I was tired of pleading . . . finally I gave up . . . ok . . . fine . . . !! If you love me . . . please slow down . . . ." I warned him.

That condition might have ringed as a warning bell in his ears . . . and he applied sudden brakes . . . I hugged him tightly and kissed him this time without his demand. After that he drove nicely. He had his share of fun by scaring me to death. I was relaxing my head on his back and enjoying the ride when something caught my attention . . . I asked him to stop the bike. We parked the bike at a side, the place was serene, as we moved the branches of trees that made a canopy and they were hiding the beauty, at back of the trees was a river flowing with mountains in the background.

I was so excited, it was like discovery of a hidden treasure, the branches of trees were hiding such a beautiful scenery, it was like a new world in this world . . . after seeing the river I just could not resist my temptation of going and feeling the flow, Maddy resisted, it might be deep he argued . . . I was reluctant and I wanted to experience, after all he had scared me and this time it was my turn so I did not listen to him and moved ahead, I knew he will not leave me alone, he too followed me. There were big rocks on which we settled ourselves. We spent time admiring nature, the sound the flowing water . . . the lush green mountain that guarded the beauty.

"Splash . . ." and before I could realize I was wet. "Maddy . . . I'm not going to leave you" I shouted and splash, splash, splash . . . Went the water . . . he stood there steady as if he was enjoying . . . I did it again, he did not even move or resist . . . So I dropped the idea, seeing that he started splashing water on me . . . We played like kids in water. I don't know for how long we played. When we started feeling hungry, we came back to the bike took our lunch bag and got settled under the big banyan tree, it was so dense and strong, we ate the sandwiches and food we had packed. We should always be prepared for worse . . . thank god I had not listened to Maddy and packed food. After that we spent time in photography; we took a lot of pictures, Maddys camera had timer setting and so we could take our pictures without anybody's help . . . I can't control my laughter thinking about the poses and weird pictures we took. All sort of funny poses that we could think of!! I know they cannot be shared with anyone . . . they are part of only our world.

After playing and clicking to heart's content, it started getting dark, we were not aware where we were so had to start the return journey else we would get lost, so we started for return. I don't know where the place was . . . but it was a splendid experience. I will cherish it throughout my life . . . .

Thanks Maddy for adding one more day full of memorable moments to my life!!

As she finished reading it she turned the page, a cute picture of theirs peeped out . . . carrying a note . . . "To add picture to our memories." Tanvi smiled seeing the picture and soon her smile turned into tears. She took the picture closer and asked Madhav in it again and again . . . "Where have you gone? Please come back? I don't know what I should do? Should I listen to Avani? What she is saying is right? You won't return? How can you be so cruel Maddy . . . how can I love you . . . How could I love a wrong person, how could I see love in your eyes? Were those deep blue eyes lying? No . . . you are not the one whom I loved . . . I hate you . . . I hate you Madhav . . ." she wept and wept till her eyes went dry and her heart saying again and again for him, Tum bin jiya jaye kaise . . . AAjao . . . lautkar phir yeh dil keh raha hai . . . later she fell asleep.

Some day after 2 months . . .

"Tannu . . . I have an idea . . . I promise this will remain a secret with me for lifetime . . . and believe me we have no other option apart from this. Listen to me patiently. Firstly I want to tell you I'm with you whatever decision you take. Now my solution to this is we will tell our parents that we are going onsite for a year from now."

"What?? I'm not going anywhere. I don't want to go . . . Why should I . . ."

"Tannu . . . I said listen to me first . . . don't interrupt . . . we are not going anywhere; we are only going to tell our parents . . . we will be here itself. After you deliver this baby, you adopt this baby."

"**Avani . . .** are you out of your senses what are you talking yaar . . . adopt my baby . . . ??? What?? I mean . . . why someone will adopt his baby . . . and . . . I mean . . . its not making any sense to me. Do you get what you are saying?"

"Listen to me . . . Tannu . . . I have a very good friend of mine who is in charge of an orphanage . . . I have talked to her . . . No no . . . She doesn't know for whom she will be doing this . . . She only knows that she has to prepare adoption papers for a child for you . . . nothing else . . . don't worry . . . she will be doing all the arrangements. After you deliver the baby she will provide us with all the legal documents of adoption. These documents will be for you to show the world you have adopted the baby. You can tell your parents and relatives that you have adopted this child after we come from onsite. In that way even they will accept the child . . . the child will get all love of relatives, grandparents and all . . . think . . . and everything will be sorted out correctly . . . I just need to know if you are ready to go with this plan. You can think on this for tonight . . . I just want to tell you . . . in this way we will get out of all the troubles and we won't harm him."

Tanvi . . . was in great confusion she nods her head in agreement and says she will think on this and tell her next morning.

Next day Tanvi is lost in her thoughts when "When you love someone you do anything, shoot out the moon . . . You do all the crazy things that you can't explain . . ." played on the radio . . .

Avani . . . came to her room . . . she took Tanvi's hand in her hand and said, "So what have you decided? Do you agree with the plan . . . Are you with me . . ."

Tanvi stared blankly at her and nodded in affirmation.

As planned they both tell their parents that they have to go to US on short notice. After a couple of months Tanvi delivers a baby boy.

In the hospital,

Finally the day had arrived when she was going to meet him . . . When she first held him in her hands she got lost in her thoughts, admiring her bundle of joy, the pain she had suffered was all worth for a glimpse of his. Their bond which was already developed got named and they were bonded together for lifetime, bonded to be there for each other. That day was the happiest day for Tanvi. His touch made her feel so complete. His voice so soft, she could now feel him close to her, as if she was holding her heart in her hands. Was this a reality she thought, she pinched herself 'oouch' . . . yes it was . . . He was near her. She could touch him, kiss him, feel his skin, his voice, she could see him smile. His tiny little hands, she took them in her hand and kissed them softly. He was so smart. Better than what she had imagined. When she looked into his deep black eyes she felt as if they were hiding the night in them with the twinkling stars peeping out of them. Everything was so perfect about him. There was nothing to deny . . . that it was what they call love at first sight. Her thought process was broken when Avani entered the room.

"Hey Tanuu . . . how are you feeling?" enquired Avani as she kept bunch of tuberose in the vase. "Ahhh . . . look at him he is so sweet . . . his skin . . . so soft . . . He looks like you Tanuu . . ."

"Lucky guy . . ." said Tanvi in excitement. After a week Tanvi was discharged from the hospital . . .

When they were back at home . . .

"Look Tannu . . . he is observing his surrounding so eagerly . . . Chikku . . . this is your home . . ." said Avani to him trying to get to his age again . . . and enjoy the moments.

"See see . . . he is so happy to come to me . . . yeah . . . chikku . . . you liked mashi na . . . hmm?? See Tanuu he is saying yes . . ." Tanvi just kept smiling back at her.

"How about calling him **Chirag**?"

"Chirag . . . huh??? great . . . I liked it . . . Chikku . . . your name will be Chiiirag . . . you get it . . . Chiiiraaag . . . he is going to be everyone's favourite . . . **Ankhon ka Tara** . . ."

"Yes . . . Chirag . . . he is the hope of my heart . . . my dream . . . my love . . ."

Tanvi and Avani got completely involved in Chirag . . . he became their first priority . . . their world had completely changed. They went shopping for Chirag. Everything revolved round Chirag. What they should buy for him and what not . . . As Chirag showed progress, every day they kept observing his each moment . . . making note of what vaccinations needed to be given to him and all . . . they kept playing with him . . . Avani and Tanvi both got involved in bringing up Chirag . . . They kept in contact with their parents daily through chat, video conferencing through skype . . . pretending to be in US.

One Day, Tanvi was in her room watering plants in the window, She was surprised to see there were two eggs laid in one pot . . . In the afternoon when Chirag was sleeping Avani came to her room. Tanvi seemed to be lost in her thoughts.

"What is little master doing? Ohhh he slept . . . So mamma is free huh??? Mamma seems to be thinking for a change huh?? What happened Tannu?"

"Avani, do you see the pigeon in that window. She laid eggs today morning . . . I'm observing both of them from morning . . . The She-Pigeon is sitting there on the pot hatching the eggs while the He-Pigeon goes out searches for sticks and brings them and gives it to her. She slowly gets up and gets holds of that stick and places it nicely on one other . . . They are preparing their nest . . ."

"So . . . What's there to be so sad in that Tanvi? It's good na . . ."

"Avani . . . they have done the same mistake as I did . . . before building their nest, before they could prepare themselves for their child, The She—Pigeon has laid eggs. But you see the He—Pigeon is with her, he is helping her build their home and up-bring their child. If birds can have that sense of responsibility and if I expected that from Maddy, was I wrong or was I expecting much from him? Is he not to the par of these birds? I'm feeling I loved the wrong person. How could I do something like this?"

"Tannu . . . look at me . . . why are you thinking about this . . . why do you want to trouble yourself . . . It was not in your hand . . . You loved the personality that he showcased to you . . . but he was not what he showed . . . You fell in love with his character, Madhav is a past. Don't do this to yourself . . . Aren't we three happy?"

"Why did I answer that wrong number Avani . . . it was a wrong number . . . not meant for me . . . Controlling her Sobs . . . I know we are happy . . . but Chirag will also need Father's love . . . protection, security, won't he?" Slowly tears started rolling on her cheek.

"Hmm yes . . . and we will give it to him . . . believe me . . ."

"One day you also have to leave us Avani . . . you will have responsibility of your own family . . . Sometimes I feel scared . . . Ma and pa will accept Chirag na??"

"Hmmm, they will; may be not at first but they will believe me . . . it might take time but they will."

As Days turned into weeks and weeks into months . . . Chirag's 1st birthday was approaching . . . they wanted to celebrate it with family . . . they both informed at home that they were coming back . . . Tanvi was very much tensed by the thought of facing her parents. But Avani convinced her . . . meanwhile they had got the adoption papers of Chirag ready . . . Tanvi wanted Avani to come with her but Avani had a point which was a fact that a person returning from US after a year will visit his home first rather than going to friend's home in some other state . . . Tanvi was convinced she has to face this situation all alone. One more thing that added to the tension was the profiles that her parents kept sending her . . . They wanted her to get married and settled. After knowing she is coming back they were all prepared to perform her marriage and then only they would leave her . . . unaware of what was stored for them. Tanvi had made up her mind she will not marry . . . She could not believe anyone after getting betrayed by Madhav . . . First love is hard to forget . . . and if you get hurt . . . it becomes harder . . . Chirag will be the only man in her life now . . . she thought to herself . . . she was bold enough to face the world and take care of Chirag all alone. May be her parents will accept her decisions after they come to know about Chirag's adoption. But she will really have tough time convincing them. All this thoughts kept creeping in her mind every now and then as she did the packing and now Tanvi was all set to face her parents.

"Give me a call any time Tannu . . . I will miss you and more than you I'm going to miss my little master . . . Chikku . . . don't forget me . . ." She said to Chirag kissing his little hand and waving good bye to them as the train left for Ernakulam—Tanvi's home town.

Chap 10

VISIT TO TVM

Tanvi visited her parents with Chirag. There was her whole family waiting to see her . . . The atmosphere at home was lively . . . small children playing around . . . all were happy and at the same time curious. They were very happy to see her after such a long time . . . Everyone gave curious looks to her and Chirag . . . understanding the questions in all eyes she told them about Chirag,

"I know you all want to know who this little champ with me is, right? Hmm so Ladies and gentlemen meet my son Chirag . . ." Tanvi announced swallowing her fear of rejection.

"Son.?" came an Obvious unanimous question back to Tanvi with eyes filled with lot of questions like how? What? When? Where?

"I know you all might be having a lot of questions, I will answer them one by one, Chirag is my adopted Son, I adopted him last year, I wanted to tell this to you so many times Appa but I could not gather courage." Tanvi went silent trying to control her sobs.

The atmosphere suddenly turned silent . . . the curiousness in eyes had turned into anger.

"Before you took such big decision, you did not think it's important to ask us once? You have become independent now . . . ? You don't need to consult parents for anything . . . huh??" Her father fired queries at her.

Tanvi had no answers to any of their questions. Everyone at home went crazy and was disappointed with Tanvi. They all turned face and moved away back to their work, they were so happy some time back but in seconds the happiness vanished, the atmosphere turned sad and dull. Tanvi knew she has to face this; she picked up her bag and started towards her room. She was tensed as she entered the house, when she reached her room her childhood memories flashed in front of her eyes. She and her brother Rudra would be whole day playing mischief and pranks, lost in her thoughts she smiled to herself, her memories gave her a comfort feeling and she knew this was her home, sooner or later her parents will accept her. She dropped her bag on floor and made Chirag comfortable on the bed, she showed Chirag all round her room and told him stories and secrets related to her room, Chirag responded with his chuckeles, Boo, hoo and hmmm sounds. "This is my study table chinu . . . you know I use to sit here and study and Rudra Mama used to sit on this chair" Tanvi said pointing to the other chair. Chirag acknowledge nodding his head and trying to catch the colorful flower in the vase kept on the table. Tanvi got busy in him thinking everything will be fine soon, but reality was tougher than what she had thought. No one was talking to her in her family. She was left alone with Chirag as if they were quarantined from the home. One day Tanvi sat in the quadrangle, while she fed Chirag, Chirag was crawling and she was following him trying her best to feed him. Chirag was busy putting his effort in trying to stand by his own holding things, He was trying to walk, Tanvi would keep appreciating his small moves. Chirag had crawled and went in the kitchen while Tanvi was lost in the song that was being played on radio "Why did you fall in love . . . Why did you break my heart . . . why did you go away . . . away . . . away . . . Dil Mera Churaya Kyu . . . jab yeh dil todna hi da . . . humse dil lagaya kyu, humse muh modna hi tha" She was brought back in present by her shouting mother, she ran in the kitchen, "Are you mad Tannu, look what you have done, if you cannot pay attention . . ." Her mom shouted at her while Chirag cried in pain, as she cleaned his hand, Tanvi's heart skipped a beat when she saw Chirag's little hand red, She was so confused what was happening. Her mother hurried and brought the first aid box, without speaking a word she applied the anticeptic and with utmost care she wrapped a bandage around it. While she was working on his wound she warned Tanvi, "Next time pay attention, he was standing there near the kitchen platform taking support of the edge, happy with his achievement when he saw those red tomatoes and he tried grasping them while he cut his hand with this knife that was lying besides. You be carefull next time you leave him alone." She finished wrapping the bandage; she cut the remaining and kissed his small hand, by now Chirag also was silent the medicine was working and the pain subsided. Her mom continued, "I will take care not to keep things in his reach . . ." realizing her changing feelings she suddenly got up keeping all things back in the first aid box. Tanvi was happy to see a change in her Mom, she was accepting them, caring for them, and she could see the love that she was hiding, the wound that caused pain to Chirag healed their relation, and she knew her mom would not be upset with her for long time. She took Chirag's hand in her and checked the wound, her heart was crying. She kissed his wound and a tear rolled down her cheek. "Im sorry my baby . . ." she whispered as she took him in her embarace and kissed his cheeks and eyes. She took him to the room and made him sleep, she slept besides him and was staring at his wound, cursing herself again when her Mom entered; she had brought milk for Chirag with turmeric powder added. But seeing him asleep she started to leave, Tanvi called out to her and holding her hand resisted to come in, she came in and sat on the bed, Tanvi was still holding her hand, she sat on her knees on the floor, "Ma, please don't be angry with me, I know I should have first taken your persmission, but please ma forgive your daughter, cannot you forgive me once, I cannot see hatered in your eyes for me ma." she kept her head on her lap and cried a lot, her mother wanted to console her, after a while of silence her mom moved her hand over her head and tugged her hair back behind her ear, pulling her face upwards by her chin she kissed her forehead, Tanvi could feel her eyes wet. She knew her Mom cannot be angry with her for long time; she slept in her lap till

Chirag let them. They were silent but the silence spoke a thousand words. When Chirag woke her mom took him in her arms and cuddled him. His soft little hands through her skin made all her anger vanish. She kissed his hands one by one and hugged him again. Tanvi felt much relaxed now, her mother had accepted Chirag and soon her Father would accept him and then everyone else. She was happy, so happy that a tear rolled down her eye on the cheek and melted down on her lips, her mom wiped her tear and hugged her, she whispered something in her ear "I had always wished my daughter to be independent, Im happy you are able to take decisions for yourself." Those words enlightened the fighting spirit in her. She hugged her mom and Chirag the trio spent some time together, it was after a long time she was spending time with her mom. When it was evening her mom hurried out of the room as it was time for Tanvi's father to return from work and he might not like seeing her in Tanvi's room. Tanvi was happy and she smiled after a long time. Thinking about her moms promise to turn her father's heart in her favor she smiled to herself and imagining her father accepting Chirag she happily carried Chirag in her arms and went round and round around herself, Chirag giggled and giggled on feeling the whirphool. Tanvi was satisfied, that day was one of the happiest days and it made her realize that the pain, tension and everything that the last year had caused in her mind and heart was worth this moment.

Next few days went in planning, how they should attack her father's anger, afterall everyone knew he was acting to be angry but he liked Chirag to be around but he did not accept that openly. Tanvi's mom had talked about this to Tanvi's grandmother, grannys are always in favor of their grandchildren not in favor of their children so it was another headcount in Tanvi's team, slowly most of the family members got added, even her brother had given in to the killing smile of Chirag and his twinkling eyes. So now the whole team had to plan and get Mogambo of the family to accept Chirag. The planning was going on and daily many plan use to come up and at the same time they use to get rejected increasing the anxiety.

Finally one day everybody came up to a common plan and they were satisfied that it will work. Everyone started working as per the plan; Sunday was decided to be the execution day.

It was early morning and Tanvi's mom had gone to temple with her brother. Her aunt and other people in home were busy in house chores. Tanvi was putting the clothes to dry in the varanda, Chirag was sleeping in his room silently, and everything was going normally. When suddenly the silent air was filled with cries of Chirag, Tanvi being in the varanda could not hear him. Her Father could hear him cry but he neglected it, after a while when no one responded to crying Chirag he got up from his chair, throwing the newspaper in anger he went in the room, Chirag was not there on the bed but he could hear his voice he looked around, he was lying on the floor, his lips were bleeding, Seeing the plight her father immediately took him and started to the family doctor. The doctor cleaned the wound and while cleaning he talked to him.

"Uncle who is this?"

"He is my grandson", without his knowledge his heart was answering the questions with pride. He was wondering, I don't like this child he repeated to himself. On the way back home he carried Chirag, He was pulling his mustache, it was something new for him, and he was playing with them, the specs. Even in pain he was smiling with his grandpa, who was trying hard to control his emotions, he had decided not to give up, but at last the loving Grandpa in him won over the angry father in him. The innocence in Chirag's eyes, his giggles and the soft touch melted all the anger in his heart. He stopped on the way and brought, sweets and some toys for Chirag, he was loaded by now. He started towards home.

While the scene at home was completely different, everyone was looking for Chirag and not finding him they were worried. Tanvi was crying and crying, everyone was worried and at that moment when they saw Chirag in his Grandpa's hands everyone was relaxed but the tension prevailed as silence was still prevelant. Everyone was shocked to see Chirag with him. Tanvi ran to her father and took Chirag from him, looking at the dressing she questioned her father, "What happened to him Appa . . ."

"He fell from the bed in sleep it seems, he was crying for a long time so I went in to see and when I saw him bleeding I took him to Mr. Bhatia" he sat to read his half read news paper pretending as if nothing has happened.

Her mom came closer to them, ". . . And what explanation do you have for the balloons and the gifts?" She questioned him.

". . . ya . . . they are . . . because . . . he . . ." Thinking and collecting words he could not answer the question and everyone burst into laughter.

"Appa, you cannot act ok; Accept it na, you love him . . ." Tanvi said hugging him from a side.

Every one was relaxed; all issues were sorted out naturally. The atmosphere turned lively. Chirag added to the happiness by his chortles and giggles. After a long time the whole family was together and it called for a celebration in name of the newly added member in the family. They all enjoyed the evening. Tanvi felt at peace after handling pressure for long time. She cried when she was alone, they were the tears of happiness of being accepted by her family. Finally everything was settled. A couple of days went by then Tanvi's parents started showing her some good prospective groom's proposals, but Tanvi denied all of them . . .

"Pa . . . I don't want to marry . . . I can live with Chirag and you have known me from childhood, I adopted him without consulting you people because I knew you won't allow me to do something like this . . . But now . . . look you all love him and I can live rest of my life all by myself, I know your concern. Like every parent you want me to get settled, you want to find the perfect partner for me who will understand me and support me . . . but I don't feel I need anyone in my life anymore . . . please let's not talk on this topic from now onwards . . . else I won't be coming here again . . . Please Pa . . . I have missed you people a lot. Let's close this topic."

Tanvi was adamant to her decision and finally her parents gave up. But they asked her to leave her job and come back home to which Tanvi promised she will be coming back home. She will try to get transferred. They all celebrated Chirag's Birthday . . . Chirag got lot of new friends with him; they included a teddy bear . . . a tortoise . . . a motor cycle . . . car. He tried to walk holding objects like table and all.

Chirag's first Birthday, It was time for Tanvi to take out some time and write down her feelings, before going to sleep she started penning down her thoughts,

Today is my prince's first birth day. But his birthday is not just a birthday for me. It is an Anniversary to celebrate; the day a year before had brought so many things in my life it was

Anniversary of our first kiss
Anniversary of our first touch
Anniversary of feeling each other
Anniversary of our eyes meet,
Anniversary of feeling complete, feeling a woman
Anniversary of my motherhood;
Celebrations of my motherhood!!
Happy B'day Chirag!!!

Thanks for giving me this chance of being your Mother—Chirag my Prince.

-Lots of love Mom.

Finally it was time for Tanvi to return. Tanvi was satisfied that finally her family has accepted Chirag.

When Tanvi came back to Pune, the big question in front of her was what next? She told Avani that she will be moving to Trivandrum, she will search for job there and since she will be closer to her home she could visit more frequently. Avani was not ready for such a decision . . . She got very upset but in the end she agreed.

"Tanvi . . . I'm always with you in all your decisions. You want to go to Trivandrum ok . . . Fine . . . But where will you live there you don't know anyone there how will you manage?"

"It's ok Avani . . . I can manage . . . it's not that hard . . . I will at least be closer to my family. It is difficult for me too to take this decision but you see . . . some time you will also have to join back to job. Once I get settled there I can call Ma there, she can take care of Chirag."

"Hmm . . . but Tannu I'm so used to you . . . how I will live without you in that house? We will be in touch, there is phone, chat, mail . . . so many things . . . but still I know I will miss you . . . but I'm letting you go . . . only for my little master's future. If you get chance do visit me . . ."

"Avani . . . I'm not leaving now . . . and do you think I won't miss you? You have been my moral support in the most difficult time of my life . . . my friend philosopher and guide . . . if I would have listened to you and not went ahead with calls on that wrong number . . . ahhhh . . . sighed Tanvi . . . let it be . . . it hurts . . . I will probably move next week . . . I came only to meet you . . . when I came here I had never thought I will get such a good friend . . . that too I will be friend with a Maharashtrian girl . . . but language never was a barrier between us . . . I will cherish all the moments we spent together Avani . . . thanks . . ."

It was time for Tanvi to leave . . . with heavy heart they both parted . . . the home Avani always looked forward to come back was no more a home . . . she used to be always in thoughts of Tanvi and Chirag. Whatever she did she saw Tanvi standing next to her . . . remembering their happy time of cooking together, washing clothes . . . doing all household chores together . . . in each corner of house she could feel Tanvi . . . After Tanvi left the house, her room was locked . . . One day Avani opened the room for cleaning and she got a high voltage shock, on the wall there was a big photo of Tanvi and Avani in a beautiful frame . . . at the end of the frame there was a letter hanging . . . Avani went closer to the frame; she moved her hand from Tanvi's face and said . . . I miss you . . . and she cried . . . with tear filled eyes she read the letter, she could not read the letter because of the water that gathered in her eyes, she hurriedly wiped her tears and started reading

My dear Pagal Friend . . .

I know dear you are missing me, before leaving I just thought to leave you with a memory of our friendship. Remember where we took this snap? ya . . . our first movie in Adlabs . . . Those were such wonderful days . . . I miss them and will cherish them always.

I don't know Avani what all is stored for us in future, we will or we may not meet. But my heart will always be caring for you and will pray for your wellbeing.

I can never forget you, the way you supported me, I don't think anyone else could. You know na . . . you are very special to me . . . and very close to my heart . . .

I wish things could happen as we want but sometimes it's not in our hands, destiny plays a major role. If I could express my feelings for you in words!! They say "A friend is someone who knows all about you and still loves you." you know all my secrets and have been with me through all those tough times, I adore you dear. You are very much more than a friend to me . . . a piece of my heart . . . How can one leave with a hole in his heart can you imagine . . . ?? But I have to . . . I have to leave now . . . acquire my independent world . . . Show this world that I'm not weak . . . no one can defeat me . . . I know you understand and you are with me in this fight of mine.

I know it's going to be hard, but please try to live in present, you will get new friends, may be better than this stupid one, who will understand you better than me. Please don't let this separation hold you back, I will never like you being held back because of me, I want you to progress, I want you to be very successful, I will pray for your success, I know you have the potential and there is much more stored for you in life . . . go and grab it, don't shed tear for we are not together . . . what does the miles have to do with our smiles huh?

You came closer to me because of my Bindass nature right, my independent nature . . . I want to see those shades of personality in you, come out of your shell and face the world. It has different shades and enjoy them, We have one life . . . don't waste it sitting and crying for me. I know what I'm saying is hard to practice and especially for us, in these years we came very close, I had never imagined I will get such a good friend or best friend . . . what should I say Avu . . . I know you caught me . . . and I have no fear in admitting this that I'm in tears right now . . . Please take care of yourself . . . I love you my cutie pie . . . and I really don't want to leave you, You are the only relation I have gained in this world . . . They say Friend is the only relation you make and I'm proud to have a friend like you in my life. Be in touch!! No need to tell you I will miss you. I know you know your value in my life . . . just wanted to tell you, I want to see you move on in life . . . If destiny permits we will meet again may be just for a while . . .

Hey . . . enough of crying yaar . . . I wanted to make you smile by my surprise . . . but see I made you cry . . . ok . . . Now wipe off those tears and get off to work . . . I will surely keep in touch with you, and even if we don't you know na . . . I'm always there in your heart and you in mine . . .

"Tera dil mera theekana . . . mera dil tera theekana . . . Tode se bhi tote na ye . . . dostana . . . humara . . ."

I will surely look to meet you in near future dear!! Smile please. Chiku will also miss you . . .

We will meet soon dear . . . don't worry . . . I will definitely come to meet you . . . now it's up to you!! when you call me . . . So marry soon . . . so we will meet soon . . . hmm . . . don't blush now . . . plan for our meeting . . . ;-)

With Loads of love,
Tannu. dt: Till our friendship lasts.

After reading the letter she felt like she should fly and reach to Tanvi . . . Avani kept spending time looking at the frame . . . she decided going home for some time which would provide a change to her . . .

Chap 11

RACING WITH TIME

Tanvi took a flat on rent in Trivandrum (TVM) and searched for job for many days, but in vain . . . then one day her door bell rings . . .

"Hello beta my name is Sam, I have a medical shop down the street, you might be knowing it! There is some problem with my computer and I came to know you work with computers can you come and check what the problem is . . ."

Tanvi was pleased to help him; she went to his shop . . . "Uncle you have a very big shop . . . but how do you manage all this . . . how do you get the stock count . . . how do you know what medicines have expired and . . ." lots of questions rose in her mind as she scanned through the shop.

"We are used to this now . . . so it is not much difficult but yes many times we go in loss because there is no proper management . . ." Tanvi looked at the age old computer being used; she was able to figure out the problem . . .

"Uncle this wire somehow got unplugged . . . I think it should boot now . . ."

"Thank you beta . . . we were so worried . . ."

Tanvi was bored being at home, She designed a small software for Sam uncle's shop which would provide proper management of what stock needs to be bought and how much quantity is needed . . . taking new requests from customers . . . printing the bills . . . and many such functionality that she thought would be useful. She gifts the software to uncle Sam, explains the details and how to operate it, uncle Sam was very much impressed . . . He thanked her for her thoughtfulness . . . Uncle Sam did a lot of publicity of Tanvi's software to his merchant friends who were whole sale retailers in varied fields . . . who were eager to buy the software. Tanvi was first reluctant to accept the amount . . . but later when Uncle Sam persuades her she accepted it as a token of love. Slowly most of the merchants in TVM started using Tanvi's software which she named "**Tavni**."

"Beta there's a spelling mistake . . ."

"No uncle I'm naming this software after my and Avani's friendship . . ."

Tanvi started getting many requests from big restaurants, malls for designing software to meet their management requirements . . . She customized it accordingly for them . . . and soon work started pouring in . . . Tanvi was not able to handle it . . . Chirag joined a play group . . . so she could give much dedicated time to her work . . . some of the colony engineering students helped her and they got to produce it as their engineering project . . . Uncle Sam provided her his godown space where they set up a small network of computers for the trainees to work . . . being trainees

Tanvi didn't pay them; all the money that she got from selling the software was a profit and the trainees got professional guidance and got to do their final year project so it was a Win—Win situation for both . . . her business cherished . . . the godown turned into a office . . . which got registered as a Pvt Ltd company "**Chirag-Desire to Excel.**" Slowly some trainees showed desire to work under her as employees . . . she started employing students . . . It did not take much time for Tanvi to get noticed by financers . . . she got good deals and her business started booming . . .

One day Tanvi was sitting in balcony reading newspaper . . . when her door bell rang . . .

"Hello . . . Madam . . . How are you . . ."

"Avi . . . OMG . . . Is this true??? Tanvi was shocked . . . You have changed so much Avani . . . 3 years . . . huh? 3 long years . . . I'm so sorry I could not come to your marriage . . . I know I disappointed you . . . But Chirag you know was not well . . ." Tanvi said pulling cheeks of little Apeksha whom Avani carried with her.

"I understand Tannu, but you will have to bear with me here, see I came here following you. Atharva is busy with his work and whenever I will feel bored I will catch you!!" Avani giggled . . .

"Not a problem dear, any time for you . . ."

They both chatted for hours, Apeksha kept them busy with her naughty smiles and cries, they talked till Chirag came back from school . . .

"Hello little Master . . . Do you know me?? Do you remember me??"

"Yes Mashi . . . Mom tells me a lot about you . . . I have seen your photo so many times . . . I know you are . . . ummm . . . Avni mashi . . . stammered Chirag. Who is she? Chjirag said pointing to Apeksha, "Your new friend" Tanvi said and Chirag smiled at her. Apeksha was too reserved to play with him; he turned to Avani and questioned, "Where is my Chocolate?" Avani gave him a Choclate and a big airplane that she had brought for him, he took it and went outside to play with it Apeksha followed him.

"How is Atharva? I mean by nature, you are happy with him na?" Tanvi enquired with concern. "I can see you are happy from the weight that you have put on", she grinned.

"I have so many things to tell you Tannu . . ." Avani was on her nerves, as if she was waiting for this moment since ages.

"So go on dear I'm all ears"

Avani started narrating her deep feelings "You know who Atharva is . . ." and she was going to continue as if she was going to open a big secret when Tanvi snapped back saying . . . "Your husband dumbo . . ."

"Aree yaar . . . not like that . . . You remember the day when we had been to Adlabs and because of that escalator thing I had dropped off my purse . . ." Avani narrated asking Tanvi to recall that day . . .

"How can I forget that day Avani . . . That was the most unfortunate day in my life . . . the day when I got call from Madhav for first time . . . I just wish that day didn't exist . . ."

"I'm sorry Tannu I did not want to hurt your feelings . . ." Avani tried to bring solace to her.

"No need for you saying sorry . . . If I would have listened to you may be I could have saved my life a disaster."

"Why Tannu don't you still love your life? Chirag is there to make all darkness in your life fade away."

"I know . . . I'm living in that one hope . . ." Tanvi said in agreement, "So what about that day . . ."

"hmmm . . . you remember that day one guy brought the wallet back to me when we were shopping"

"ahh . . ." Tanvi tried to recall and when she did she replied, "Yes I remember, nice guy he had come running after he saw you to return your wallet."

"By any chance you remember his name?" Avani questioned.

"No yaarr . . . Avu . . . you stop this quiz session and come to the point. "

"ok ok . . . chill . . . that guys name was Atharva . . ."

"So . . .", Tanvi was irritated by now . . . but when she realized what Avani was saying, "You mean your Atharva is that guy?" Avani nodded as if she let out a big secret. "Avani . . . you bitch . . . you didn't even tell me you are having an affair . . . and how stupid of me to believe you . . ." Tanvi started complaining and hitting Avani, Avani ran to other side of the sofa and asked her to cool down, "Tannuu please listen to me . . . affair and all . . . nothing like that yaar . . . I will continue only if you listen to me in peace."

"Ok . . . go on . . ." Tanvi said settling in the sofa getting a pillow and Avani continued, "Yes, he is the same guy but it's not a love marriage but an arranged cum love marriage . . . Atharva's parents had come to my place to see me and it was all done in traditional way while Atharva was in US for some assignment, you know na how conservative I'm, I had not even seen his pic, I was just going to follow whatever my mom dad decide. His parents forwarded my profile to him after giving their confirmation." Avani went silent for sometime . . . "Madam come out of your memories and let me also know what happened next . . ." Avani was blushing as she narrated Tanvi, "hmm then one day all of a sudden I got a call from him, I had not even seen him but he thought I have seen him so he talked in that context as if we know each other . . .", Avani was smiling to herself remembering her first conversation with Atharva Tanvi teased her . . . "Oye hoye . . . then . . . then what happened . . ." Avani moved Tanvi's hand from her cheek and continued . . . "Then nothing we had calls and mails and soon started developing interest and then we got married . . . then Apeksha . . ." Tanvi kept staring at her listening to her fast forward story . . .

"No way . . . this is not done . . . I'm not accepting this . . . you have to tell me in detail . . ." Tanvi declared.

"What details yaar . . . ???" Avani asked innocently . . . "Aree you just told me so plainly . . . no spice in the story . . ." Tanvi moved closer to Avani and said, "I want to hear it with all the spice in it . . . ya don't show that innocent face to me as if you are not getting what I'm saying . . . If you want me to say it straight ok . . . I want to hear about your First kiss . . . then about $@^%&@ all that you know"

"What Tannu . . . are you mad . . . how can I narrate these things . . ." Avani blushed . . .

"Ohh really and what about you bugging me all the time asking me what I did with Madhav . . . that too in details hmm?? How you wanted to know if he took my hand in his and what we spoke, ohh God you were so, now I hope you realize how difficult it is huh . . . so I'm all ears . . ." Tanvi teased her again . . . Avani realized that she has no escape from her and she has to tell her all details . . .

She tried escaping herself from the beating that she was getting from Tanvi with the pillow, she moved to the other sofa and got a pillow for herself and soon started a pillow fight between them. They hit as hard as they could to each other. After a while both were tired and they relaxed on the sofa. Soon Tanvi regained her energy and said, "You are not spared dear you have to tell me the whole thing . . ." she grinned at Avani and was about to throw the pillow at her when Avani squeaked, "Time please!" Regaining her energy, she went in the kitchen and got a bottle from freeze, sipping water she nodded at Tanvi trying to tell her she quits and will tell her every detail, a great smile of conquer could be seen on Tanvi's face. After a while when they were back in form Avani started narrating, "So you know after that call we kept taking daily, he would call me and I would wait for his call, just like you did for Maddys call . . ." Avani spoke the truth in a flow and then realized what she said; she looked at Tanvi . . . "Im sorry Tannu but you know whenever I used to be with Atharva you know I always remembered the good times you narrated with Maddy . . . I missed you both I know what he did is so bad but for some reason when Atharva did something nice for me I would remember Maddys love towards you . . . You know I was not telling anything of this to you for this one reason. Because all this will make you remember him, I know you so well . . . ." Avani was in tears realizing she has hurt her.

Tanvi shifted towards her and holding her hand in hers she softly tried to speak controlling her emotions, "Yes Avani it hurts! But nothing is in our hands right? I have learnt to live in the present. Past cannot be changed and I don't want to spend rest of my life crying. I have come over all this and you don't worry I'm strong enough to keep my past memories locked, you can speak all your heart to me, I know there are many things you want to tell me . . .", she smiled and encouraged her, Avani smiled back to her.

"Ya Tannu you know I use to feel so lonely when I had a fight with Aatthy"

"What Aatthy huh, so now I know what you call him . . ."

"Tannu . . ." Avani tried to cry like a baby . . .

"Ok ok, continue . . . I'm going to keep mum now."

"hmm . . . that's better . . . ok so what should I tell you . . . ok ha . . . you know on our first valentine I got a big surprise, I was in office and I got call from dispatch section that I have a courier, I was unaware of what was stored for me, I went to collect it, when I read the from section it had US address but me idiot still did not understand that it was parcel sent by him . . . I came back to desk and opened it . . . there popped a teddy out of it with a rose and a message saying "You are permitted to hug him till the time I'm there." there was a big card in it, my first card you know the one that has all those lovely words . . . I just loved this surprise and I too wanted to do something for him thanks to the IT revolution and these days you can send gifts within no time in any part of the world but I had to prepare from thinking what to send and how to send . . . I just copied his idea . . . I thought of sending him a cute very similar kind of teddy but then I thought guys don't like teddy . . . a bottle of Beer? But then I got another nice idea . . . I recorded his most fav songs in my voice the romantic one and sent him the CD with a card, he loved it and he told me that he watched the CD at least once every day, he had timed it to auto play with his alarm, so the first thing that he saw in morning was me . . . and what he heard was my voice . . . I just loved that feeling, these caring ways of his . . . I don't know when I started getting dependent on him, if for some reasons he would not call I would get so impatient I would not get sleep . . ." While Avani was narrating Chirag came in complaining . . . "Mamaa . . . Apeksha is not listening to me . . ." Apeksha came and clinged to Avani. They both consoled them and tried to put them to sleep, After they slept as they shifted to the bedroom, Avani looked at the watch it was very late, "I had asked Atharva to come at 8 its 10 he is still not here" Avani looked worried. Tanvi asked her to stay at her place and inform Atharva about that, Avani took her cell and called Atharva, "We got so engrossed in our chat I just didn't pay attention to the time . . .", Avani complained as she heard the bell ring on the other side, "Hey Avani . . . sorry dear was in a meeting and got late will catch you in some time on my way . . ." Avani smiled to herself realizing his ways to convince her before she says anything to him . . . "hmm I know . . . its ok . . . ok listen Aatthy I'm staying at Tannu's place today so you don't come, I will come on my own tomorrow morning . . . ok?"

"No . . . if you sleep there then what about me . . . you can't do this to me jaan . . ."

"Hmmm nothing doing take is as punishment for getting late . . ." Avani said in a naughty tone.

"Ya ya who is going to care about this nacheez when her best friend is with her . . ." Atharva nitpicked.

"Stop your Drama now, have good food and go to sleep" Avani instructed him.

"You mean you have cooked food for me? Means this was preplanned . . . ??? I know you are gossiping about me to your friend . . ."

"Stop it Aatthy . . . there are good restaurants at walkable distance from our house have food and go to sleep will give you a wakeup call tomorrow morning ok?"

"Do I have any option? Ok . . . you carry on . . . but don't complain about me much to your friend huh?"

"You very well know I'm not complaining, you can ask Tannu later when you meet in person. Chalo then see you ok . . . bye . . . GN . . ."

"Ok dear will not take much of your time. Will be waiting to see you tomorrow morning, Love you a lot!" Atarva said throwing a kiss at her. Avani blushed and just replied "Me too!!" and disconnected the call. Tanvi was putting blanket over Chirag and Apeksha and while they were sleeping comfortable she made herself relax at one side of the bed . . . Avani came on the other side and rolling blanket over herself in husk voice she replied to Tannu, "I told him I will come tomorrow morning."

"You could have called him here na . . . I would have met him . . ." Tanvi replied in a lower tone.

"No he would have not let us speak . . . he is a big chatter box . . . we would have to listen to him all time" Avani grinned . . .

"So you mean we have all the time for ourselves now? So I'm all years you can continue dear . . . ." Tanvi gave her a wide smile.

"Yes we have the whole time . . ." and she started telling her all things that were kept locked in her heart from such a long time. They talked whole night in husk voice in fear that Chirag and Apeksha might wake up. They talked and talked the whole night sometimes by eyes sometimes with hand signal the two on the sides of bed with Chirag and Apeksha sleeping in between.

Somewhere at sunrise they slept for a while.

After marriage Atharva tried for transfer to Pune from TVM as Avani's company did not have a center in TVM, but in vain, So Avani resigned. Avani was tired of her housewife routine . . . Avani joined Tanvi in her business, With Avani Tanvi loved her work a bit more; they both worked hard and took the business to new heights. They open 3 branches of their office in different parts of TVM in 3 years. Tanvi got interviewed as inspiring women of India . . . her interviews were published in leading newspaper. A small town girl created so much of employment . . .

After a year, she was being interviewed on national television for a famous show called **'Kiran'** . . . Show about people who have brought ray of hope in many lives . . . there were questions asked to her about who was her role model and what inspired her . . . the history of her company '**Chirag.**' Her struggle and many more typical interview type questions . . .

A deep blue pair of eyes were watching this show . . . after watching the show . . . they got Tanvi's no from the channel office . . .

A no is being dialed on the mobile . . . the pair of eyes keep staring at the no . . . Someone answers the call . . .

"Hello . . . Is Ritu There??" said the voice.

"Sorry wrong number." Answered Tanvi and disconnected the call. After disconnecting the call Tanvi realized . . . who it was on the call . . .

~ Thoughts to ponder ~

Yes . . . you guessed it right . . . It is Madhav who called her . . . but . . .

1. Why did he call her after such a long time . . . 5 years is a long time . . . ??
2. Does he want to black mail her? After seeing her success? After knowing about Chirag? What is more stored for Tanvi? Good or bad?

All these are going to be answered . . . keep reading . . . for more . . .

Chap 12

THE RESTLESS CALL

The call made Tanvi restless . . .

"Why did you break my heart . . . why did you fall in love . . . why did you go away . . . Dil mera churaya kyu . . . jab ye dil todna hi tha . . . humse dil lagaya kyu, humse muh modna hi tha . . ."

As if all the sadness that she kept hidden from herself started finding their ways to her heart, her mind was overcrowded with thoughts and questions . . . heart was filled with emotions . . . she could not find answer to any of the question and at the same time she did not know what should be done next. She called up Avani, "Avani . . . Avi . . . Ma . . . Madhav . . . Madhav called me . . . you please come home . . ." she could speak only this, and she burst into tears.

"Tanuu . . . what . . . what are you saying . . . ok . . . ok I'm on my way will be there in 15 min . . . ok . . ."

Avani reached Tanvi's place, Tanvi was staring at the ceiling . . . "Tanuu . . . are you all right . . . what did he say?"

"He didn't say anything . . . Someone had called me asking for Ritu . . . I know it's him . . . same voice . . ."

"Then? What did you say?"

"I . . . I . . . realized it's him after disconnecting the call." She hugged Avani and kept weeping. "Avani . . . why did he call me now . . . after so many years? What does he want from me now? I won't give Chirag to him . . . I don't want anything from him . . . I just don't want to talk to him. I will go mad thinking why he called after so many years."

"Show me your mobile . . ." Avani looked in call directory it was a mobile no. "Tannu . . . do you want me to call him and ask?"

"No Avani . . . forget it . . . I just don't want to get involved this time; forget it." A few days passed and both forgot about it . . .

One day Tanvi was returning home, she saw Madhav sitting on a stone under a tree near her building . . . She kept watching his moves . . . he also noticed her . . . and stood there . . . he kept waiting for her to come; he was stand still . . . Tanvi kept walking but her speed decreased as her thoughts increased . . . Just when Madhav thought about talking to her Tanvi took a turn and went away . . . Madhav was not able to understand her behavior . . . he waited there thinking; He saw Avani coming from the other side looking for space to park her car . . . he went running to her . . .

"Hey Avani . . ." he said panting trying to catch with her car speed.

Avani gave him a blank stare, she didn't respond and left.

Madhav kept waiting for Tanvi . . . Tanvi saw him at same place next day . . . today Chirag was playing with him, that view ignited anger in her, she tried to keep calm, when Chirag came back he rushed into his room, Tanvi followed him shouting at him, "Chirag, how many times have I told you, you should not talk to strangers?"

"Yes Mamma I know, I don't talk to strangers . . ." Chirag innocently replied while he was busy searching for something.

"I saw you were talking to that man sitting under the tree, didn't you?" Tanvi was out of control.

"Look mom that uncle prepared this boat for me, and see this is helicopter and frog" Chirag showed her different paper made crafts that Madhav taught him, he was very excited and wanted to try them out himself . . . he kept searching and finally found the craft book, with that he got busy and he didn't listen to anything that tanvi spoke, warning him Tanvi left the room, "I don't want you to talk to him again . . . ok?"

She was busy with the dinner preparations when something came and hit her head, she looked around for it and it was a helicopter, Chirag was playing with it, she was angry but when she saw how happy he was for creating his first helicopter she didn't say anything, it was not flying properly because it didn't have the finishing touch, Chirag came running to her to get his helicopter and with that he complained to her, "Mamma this is not flying properly . . ."

Tanvi sat down with him and showed him how he should have made it and after correcting a few turns of the paper and sharpening the turns the helicopter took a great flight . . . Chirag clapped his hands witnessing his first helicopter flying, when it landed he picked it up and with it in his hands he ran all round the house making sounds like "zoom . . . zoom . . . zoooooooooooooom"

Tanvi just appreciated him and was back to her preparations. They had food and finally Chirag went to sleep he kept the helicopter to his bedside, it was his favorite toy.

Next day after coming from school, he went to Madhav and showed him his helicopter and proudly displayed it to him how high it was flying and all, Madhav appreciated him for his work and asked him do you want to learn something new today, Chirag looked at him with suspicious eyes, thought for a while and before he replied Madhav asked him for his drawing book, then with the help of a thread and ink he showed him different designs that he could draw, mixing colors and how to choose colors. Chirag was so happy to see the flowers in yellow and blue color, he took the thread from Madhava and tried doing it himself, Madhav took hold of his tiny hands and guided him to place the thread in particular manner and then he folded the paper and removed the thread and poof . . . the flower was drawn . . . Chirag clapped in excitement and jumped on his place . . . "one more one more", he shouted delighted "ok . . . this time we will make a butterfly ok?"

"Butterfly . . . wow . . . will that fly like my Helicopter?" Chirag questioned him imagining a beautiful butterfly flying around.

"If you ask him to fly he will!" smiled Madhav.

Again with his expert hands Madhav placed the thread on the paper and in mins there was a beautiful butterfly seeing which Chirag was happy, "Now ask him to fly", he ordered Madhav, Madhav took his craft scissor and cut the butterfly and then he tied a thread to it, like a kite he flew it, Chirag was jumping in joy seeing the butterfly fly, he ran to him and took hold of the string and with it he ran around the street, he was engrossed running with the butterfly and didn't realize he was running on the road, his joyous heart came to a standstill when he bumped against a car and he fell down. Tanvi got out of the car and tensed she went to see him; he was not hurt much, Tanvi started bombarding him, "How many times have I told you not to play on the road huh?" scolding and dragging him by his right hand she took him back home, She cleaned his hurt ankle and applied medicine, Chirag shouted on the pain to which Tanvi sarcastically commented, "This will remind you not to play on road henceforth." Chirag was silent and he kept blowing air on the ankle to get relief, suddenly he recollected something and he ran back to the road, Tavi kept calling him to come back, he was back in some time and he showed Tanvi his flying butterfly, Tanvi was exultant to see him so full of excitement. She brushed his hair and participated in his excitement and casually asked, "Who made it?" "That uncle" Chirag said pointing to Madhav from window. A sudden unhappiness covered Tanvis face, "I told you yesterday na not to talk to strangers? You don't understand what Mamma says?"

"But mamma that uncle is very nice, he showed me how to draw flower with thread." Chirag pleaded to which Tanvi did not hear.

Next day Tanvi woke up with a little headache, she prepared hot coffee for herself and getting lost in the aroma she went to the living room, she kept the cup at the table and went to get the paper, reading the headlines she separated the window curtains and sat next to the window, she took the cup in one hand and was engrossed in reading the news when a sight disturbed her, while reading in between she gazed through the window and there she could see him, Madhav was sleeping on a wooden log with a blanket wrapped around, for a while her heart experienced high pitch pain all thoughts of his wellbeing came to her mind, the night was very cold he seemed to be weak, had he had his dinner all thoughts came in a sudden gush to her mind, but soon the feeling was taken over by hatred, As she watched over him she could see he was awake, he tried and with support of the log he sat beside the tree, he looked pathetic with the swollen eyes and the beard, Tanvi was lost observing his moves when Avani entered

"Avani . . . ask him to leave . . . I don't want to talk to him . . . please ask him to leave me alone . . .", Tanvi pleaded to Avani trying to hide her pain. Avani consoled her and said, "I will talk to him."

Avani reached out to Madhav, "Madhav . . . listen to me carefully . . . I'm here only to tell you that Tanvi doesn't want to talk to you . . . please leave us alone . . . we have faced a lot and we don't want to see any more . . . life has taught us lot . . ." while she was busy shooting at him she noticed he has grown weak and he was coughing, he was not well and needed immediate medical assistance, Avani could not see him in this state, she understood that it is because of spending the cold nights on the streets that made Madhav's health pathetic, she wanted to help him but the past did not allow her she kept looking at him, Madhav tried to speak and convince her, "Avani . . . please . . . I need one chance . . . I just want to talk to her once . . . please . . . only one favor . . . Avani please . . . I came here in search of only that one chance . . ."

"Look Madhav . . . you don't know what we have gone through . . . what is it that brings you here after 5 years? Does it take 5 years to realize you love someone? When it's not convincing enough to me how can I convince Tanvi??? no way . . . just go away Madhav . . . there's no place for you here . . . please don't treat yourself this way and don't hurt yourself as I know it hurts Tanvi to see you like this . . ."

"Avani . . . one chance . . . I will leave after that . . ." Madhav said breaking Avanis sentence in between.

"You promise you will leave after that?" Avani Asked for assurance.

"Yes . . . I want to talk to her once . . . Please . . ." plead Madhav.

"Ok . . . I will try . . . This is only because at some point of time I believed in you . . . And I want to see Tanvi happy."

"Thanks Avani." Madhav waited in hope to see Tanvi.

Avani persuaded Tanvi to talk to him for once . . . even after lot of efforts Tanvi was not ready . . . It was again a cold night; Tanvi put Chirag to sleep and went by the window to close it . . . There she saw him again . . . sitting by the road . . . her heart cried . . . but neglecting her feelings she closed the window. It rained heavily that night; Tanvi could not sleep the whole night . . . She kept staring at the window blankly, hoping he was doing well, The restlessness in her kept rising . . . finally she decided to talk to him next day . . . at least she had the right to abuse him . . . she thought to herself. He had no right to torture her this way even when she was not at fault. Next day when Tanvi was coming back from office she saw Chirag standing next to Madhav who was being examined by doctor, Last night was heavy for him, after examining and giving him some tablets Doctor left, Tanvi was standing there at a side while Chirag made him sleep and covered him with blanket, she went closer to him and he tried to sit and talk to her . . . Tanvi kept looking straight in his eyes . . . tried to control her emotions; she kept mum for some time . . . both were silent for a while then Madhav broke the silence . . .

"Tannu . . . I just wanted to tell you that . . ."

"Look Madhav . . . I don't want to create a scene here . . . please let me live or you can't even see me alive? It's not bearable to you that even after destroying my life . . . I pounced back and I'm successful today? What is your problem? Just leave us alone . . . we don't need you . . . what on earth has brought you to me after 5 years?"

"Tannu . . . listen to me please . . ."

"Look mister my name is Tanvi . . . and I don't talk to strangers . . . this is my 1st and last warning to you after this you will see the jail . . ." saying Tanvi went away dragging Chirag with her.

After reaching home Chirag got a share of his bashing for calling the doctor and giving him the blanket, Tanvi was not able to understand Chirag's behavior. She tried to keep him away from Madhav.

Madhav was sitting at his usual place on the wooden log, lost in his thoughts, he was thinking about Tanvi and his relation, the incidents kept running in front of his eyes and he was relieving them again, engrossed in them he could feel the same feelings again the nth time he lived them in his mind, one such incident that played disturbed him, Tanvi looked awefull. She was angry on him for making her wait for 5 min. Madhav smiled to himself recollecting the incident. Tanvi had not talked to him for the whole day, just because he was late by 5 min, but later she had told him she was dying to talk to him every sec. He loved that feeling of belonging that she had for him. Suddenly he realized how much pain he might have caused her by making her wait for 5 long years, that Tanvi who could not bear a delay of 5 min, how she might have coped with her life in these 5 years. The thought made Madhav fidgety, the pain he had caused her, the realization that he has hurt her made him restless. His heart was crying, he knew he has to do something to make up. But Tanvi was not ready to listen to him and that was making the situation worse. Tanvi has changed so much, he thought to himself, Earlier she would come and give him a warm hug whenever they met. Today she was not even ready to see him, talking was out of question. He was spending days in only one hope to get one chance to talk to her. Lost in his thoughts he went to sleep.

Chap 13

LETTER FROM MADHAV

A day later, Chirag came home with a paper in his hand . . .

"Mamma . . . this is for you. That uncle gave this to me to give you", said Chirag pointing to Madhav on the road in his childish voice . . .

"Why did you go to him again? I told you not to talk to him right?" Tanvi snached the paper from him and she was fuming inside . . . She tore the letter into pieces and threw it into dustbin . . . digesting her anger she asked Chirag to complete his homework. He could sense her anger and silently he sat to do his homework. Without uttering a word he completed his homework. Tanvi prepared dinner banging utensils to show her anger and frustration. They had dinner and went to sleep . . . The harder she tried to forget him his thoughts troubled her, she wanted to sleep and wake up to know all this was a bad dream. She tried diverting her mind and think about the issues they were facing in office but in vain, he mind was constantly gazing the dustbin, what might be in the letter, she thought to herself. She convinced herself that whatever it was she was not interested in this anymore and she was happy with her life. She closed her eyes and tried to get some sleep, but she could not sleep and she kept changing sides whole night . . . finally she decided to read it . . . she went to the kitchen, collected the pieces of letter, and tried reassembling the pieces and put an effort reading it, In her anger she tore it into really small pieces it was like playing a jigsaw puzzle but she knew she will not be able to sleep unless she reads it so her determination paid and she had the letter in front finally . . .

She took a deep sigh and started reading it

Tanvi,

I thought for a long time what should I write but I could not add any adjective to your name, maybe I don't have that right. One last time please listen to me . . . after this you will have answers to all your questions.

It was a stormy day . . . I could sense it . . . Sea was signaling me about an unseen danger . . . but I neglected the thought about danger . . . I did not want any disturbance between you and me . . . listening to "Kyu chalti hai pawan . . . kyu aati hai bahar . . . kyu hota hai pyaar . . . Na tum jano na hum . . ." I was gazing the sky at our special pair of stars . . . which made me feel you are with me . . . I was deep in my thoughts when my ship experienced a big bolt that shook me . . . people started running . . . everyone was shouting, the calm atmosphere changed into aggressive in a moment . . . After some investigations I came to know, we were attacked by pirates and to add to havoc we were not prepared for this situation. We were not having enough ammunition and manpower to overcome such crisis situation as a result we were defeated . . . most of my fellows were dead, somehow I with my other 10 fellows escaped from the ship . . . we were swimming directionless for almost 2 days, the water was chilling cold . . . I don't know when how, I had lost my consciousness, when I regained I was stranded on an Island. It was a breath taking experience. we saw some hope of survival; else I could only see water for 2 days and we were tired of swimming. But the do or die attitude in us kept us moving . . . we had to face many adverse situations which are not worth mentioning . . . we were only 8 on the island. We were sure enough that our search team was on their way to find and help us. We lived on this hope that someone will come for our rescue for about four months . . . The watch that you gave me kept telling me, time is ticking . . . and it created a lot of pain . . . We had nothing with us, absolutely nothing to contact someone to ask for help . . . we lived on hope that some ship or airplane going through will notice us and help us . . . but then finally . . . we decided we have to move on and find our way . . . We started collecting wood . . . Everything needed to be reinvented it was like we were into stone age . . . right from our tools to every nail that we wanted to use we had to build it on our own . . . but your love kept me going . . . We ate whatever we found on the land, and worked day and night . . . half of the wood that we collected needed to be burnt at night in order to protect ourselves from cold and wild animals. But after 6-8 months we had a boat in front of us that could accommodate 5 people in it. Yes we lost 3 friends.

That day my joy knew no bounds . . . I was going to meet you . . . but then again we met with a problem . . . which direction do we sail? Again . . . you helped me . . . I kept sailing in the direction of my special star . . . it was the only guide. Finally after sailing for days, one day we saw a ship, after convincing them about our condition they agreed to help us, with their help we reached Indonesia, their destination, my clock showed I travelled for 8 months . . . After a long process which involved lot of communication and high level interactions we got considerations and arrangements were done for us to leave for India . . . again I saw a ray of hope. I reached Delhi, I had to work day and night there to collect money to get ticket for Pune; I worked as a worker in a factory there, and after 3 months finally I had my ticket to Pune in hand . . . Tears were rolling on my cheeks that day Tanvi . . . I swear . . . but in the train I just kept thinking about you . . . "Jab ek ladka ek ladki se milta hia pehli baar . . . toh kya hota hia . . . bolo yaar . . ." After listening to this song playing on my neighbors mobile I went in my world . . . our first meeting . . . and I didn't even realize when I reached Pune. I went direct to your home, but I could not find anyone there, my heart skipped a beat. But I was positive . . . I thought you might have been to your home I kept visiting daily but in vain . . .

Then one day I read your interview in newspaper . . . my heart again longed to live . . . but my joy was of fraction of sec . . . I came to know you named your company after your son . . . I broke into pieces . . . I thought to myself . . . and somewhere I felt you did it right . . . it was hard to accept but . . . till when could you wait for me and then your parents might have pressurized you for marriage . . . so it was none of your fault . . . I accepted the truth . . . I never wanted to interfere and come back in your life and create disturbance . . . But a few days back I saw your interview on TV in that I came to know that Chirag is your adopted son . . . I enquired about you at the channel, then, I came to know the reality . . . I took the 1st ticket for TVM and came here . . . but you were not ready to listen to me . . . I just wanted one chance; I wanted to tell you the truth. This is the truth, I know you hate me . . . you might be thinking my promises were false . . . but Tannu . . . sorry . . . Tanvi I did not get a chance to prove myself to you . . . I just wanted the truth to come into light.

If it would have been in my hands I would have placed you in my place and let you know how much you mean to me, how much I love you, how dear I hold you to this heart, how valuable you are and how much you mean to me . . . if only I could do this and place you in my place . . . if we could interchange our roles. But I know I'm at fault, may be this was my destiny to love you, to get you and then lose you forever. It's not your fault Tannu, whatever you did is right, moving on in life is the only thing we can do, but without you I cannot move a single bit . . . till today I lived on a hope to see you, I have seen you, you are happy and so now am I. Aim of my life is fulfilled, I'm happy for me and just want to tell you, I will love you even after I'm gone. Just keep this in mind, I always loved you in the past and will love you in the future of time, where ever I might be. Take care of yourself.

If only things would have been in my hands . . . I would have showed you how much I love you . . . and what you mean . . .

I was always thinking ahead, making decisions soaked with fear . . . Today, because of you . . . because of what I learned from you; every choice I made was different and my life has completely changed . . . it doesn't matter if you have five minutes or fifty years I value it only if I'm with you. Tannu if not for you today, if not for you I would never have known love at all . . . So thank you for being the person who taught me to love . . . and to be loved. I want to hold on to you as I know once you loved me with all your heart and I have broken your trust, but I still love you with whole of my heart and I long for that one smile from you. I wish you success for your future. I'm happy to see you successful; I will always be there with you forever.

I always believed GOD created spaces between my fingers so that one day they can be filled by yours.

"Ye zamin aasaman, yeh chaman ye jahan kuch rahe na rahe . . . pyaar toh hamesha rahega . . . Mere dil mein kon hai dhadkano mein kon hai . . . kon hai nazar mein . . . ?? **Sirf tum . . . .**"

I waited for you, for one chance for 5 days . . . but I can't give more pain to you. I'm leaving. Bye.

Always and only yours,
Maddy.

"Hum bewafa hargiz na the . . . . par hum wafa kar na sake . . ."

After reading the letter Tanvi was shattered . . . It was dawn by the time Tanvi realized, She rushed to the window to get a glimpse of him . . . but she could not find him anywhere around there.

Qs: Will she find him?

Chap 14

The Past Returns

Tanvi ran down the stairs . . . she reached next to the stone where Madhav used to sit . . . she was moved, on the stone she found it carved . . .

"Look into my eyes you will see, what you mean to me . . . search your heart search your soul . . . when you find me there you search no more . . ." Tanvi was left with Tears and only tears . . . she collapsed down . . . hugged the stone and cried and cried . . . uncontrolled . . . she kept talking to herself . . . asking him to come back . . . but in vain . . . he was gone . . .

"Mujhse hui baas ye khata . . . maine tujhe chaha sanam . . . chup chup ke roti rahi, tune diye kaise ye gaam . . . o bekhabar beraham karle chahe jitney sitam na chahat hogi kabhi kam muzhe in aaoosuoon ki kasam . . . maine kiya hai tuzhse saccha pyaar . . ."

After some time Avani came there . . . she took Tanvi back home . . . read the letter . . . after knowing the truth . . . she was in tears . . . she hugged Tanvi . . . both cried . . .

Avani consoled her . . . "Don't worry Tannu we will find him . . . come let's move . . ." said Avani and she dragged Tanvi to the door.

"He left Avi . . . he won't come back . . . he doesn't want to hurt me . . . but does he know how much pain this has caused to me?"

"He might be in the city itself . . . don't worry . . . you have his mobile . . . dial that no and see if he answers . . ." Tanvi found a hope . . . she dialed the no . . . but it was not reachable . . . "Avani . . . I hope he doesn't take some extreme step . . . I have hurt him . . . he has no one other than me in this world . . . I cannot imagine what he might be going through . . . He has also suffered for these 5 years na . . . and it was none of his fault . . . I hope he is safe . . ." Tanvi disclosed her fear . . . remembering the line from his letter aim of my life is over . . .

"Tanvi . . . think positive . . . He is strong . . . He lived these years thinking you are gone but now when he can see there is a chance of you accepting him . . . he won't do anything stupid . . . this cannot end like this . . . we will find him . . . I know!! It was not the wrong number Tannu . . . It was the right number and it was connected by GOD . . . So relax . . . just keep looking . . . we will find him . . ." assured Avani. Avani called Atharva and narrated the whole incident to him, he left from his office immediately, and they divided the areas and started looking for Madhav. Atharva called Avani from time to time and asked her to take care of Tanvi. Tanvi was no way in her senses she only wished one thing and that was to see him once, she wanted to feel him again, witness his smile.

The roads were blocked due to damage caused by heavy rains in the city last night, there was havoc and accidents at every corner people running here and there for help, Tanvi's heart was somewhere telling her everything was going to be allright, this cannot end this way, but her mind was challenging her, all bad thoughts came to her mind, she was restless and the fight between her mind and heart was killing her, she felt as if her heart was loaded and it could burst any moment. She was physically present with Avani but she was with him in her dream world, They searched all railway stations, bus stops and airports . . . even hospitals . . . but they were not able to find him . . . They were back to home in the evening tired, Avani went to park the car . . . Tanvi was waiting for het at the gate when she saw a blurred image of a man walking on the other side, it was dark all around, though she could not see him properly something inside her told her it's Madhav . . . she ran behind him and reached to him and stopped him . . . took a look at him . . . Yes . . . it was him . . . her heart skipped a beat . . . he had a flex of hair waving on his face . . . the same deep blue eyes but no sparkle in them and no smile on lips . . . Tanvi gave him a tight slap and then hugged him tightly . . .

"You Idiot . . . how dare you leave me? I waited for you for 5 years . . . you could not wait for 5 days?" Tightening her embrace . . . "Don't ever leave me again . . ."

Madhav hugged her back . . . "I promise I will never . . ." They looked at each other . . . Madhav tugged her hair back, feeling touch of her skin . . . He passionately kissed her forehead. Then loosening his embrace, he looked in her eyes and said **"I love you!"**

she took his hand in her, she filled spaces between his fingers by hers, looked at him and said . . "I hate you", Madhav looked at her with wide eyes . . . "he he he . . . I love you too, my dumboo . . ." she said giggling . . . Madhav kept looking at her in amazement . . . then she passionately kissed his hand back . . . they were lost in each other.

"Tum ho toh gata hai dil . . . tum nahi . . . toh geet kaha . . . tum ho toh hai sab hasil tum nahi . . . toh kya hai yaha . . . tum ho to hai sapno ke jaisa haseen ek sama jo tum ho toh ye lagta hai mil gayi har khushi, jot tum na ho toh lagta hai ke har kushi main hai kami . . . ye tumko hai maangti ye zindagi . . . tum nahi toh kuch bhi nahi . . . Jo tum ho toh hawawo ko bhi mohabatoo ka rang hai . . ."

By that time Avani reached there; Chirag, who was playing nearby, saw his mother cry and he also reached there.

Looking them come they both turn to them, "Thanks Avani . . . I cannot explain what you have done for me . . . I owe my life to you . . . and . . . also to you dear . . ." picking up Chirag in his arms he looked at Tanvi and said, "Your son is very sweet Tannu . . . He brought me food daily . . . we used to chat daily . . . gave me a blanket . . . he is very sweet . . . just like you . . . ummm I think kinder than you . . . I developed a strange bond with him in these 5 days . . ."

"May be . . . He could not see his father suffer . . ." Hearing this Madhav rolled his eyes . . . raising his eyebrows . . . "Yes . . . He is not my Son . . . he is your Son . . . **Our** Son . . ."

Avani carried Chirag with her and left the two together to share their stories, to share the love and pain that was left untold for these many years "I had no other option Maddy, I did not have courage to kill my love, that time I believed you betrayed me; you too were just like the others behind physical pleasures. I hated you so much or I hated myself so much for loving a wrong person. I cursed everyday myself for judging you wrong, I could not believe what was happening with me but some day I had to accept the reality, I had tried everything that was in my hand but this was something that even if I wanted I could not have kept a secret. So I and Avani came up with the adoption plan. I was left with no other option Maddy . . . ."

Tanvi told him the complete story. She rested her head on his chest and let the tears flow . . . let the pain that she carried in her heart for all these years get away, so that she can create room for love, love that was so pure and it was her love that had brought Madhav back to her . . . Madhav caressed her hair, he was silent, though it was none of their fault they both had experienced their share of pain, the separation was their destiny. He could feel the pain Tanvi went through. He got sad and was speechless; he wiped her tears and gave a soft hug, then kissing her forehead he said, "I will never leave you henceforth dear . . . I'm always with you, I'm sorry for causing pain to you." Tanvi surrendered herself in his arms; they sat there for a while. Controlling her sobs Tanvi uttered some words . . ." It has been 5 years now that I met you, but even now I remember everything from that year of our first meeting, down to the smallest details. When I feel lonely, when I feel your need I relive that year often in my mind, bringing it back to life those moments we spent together they had so much life in them that they add life to me even today, inspire me to live, and When I relive them I realize that, I always felt combination of sadness and joy. Sometimes I wish I could roll back the clock and take all the sadness away and have you just there in my arms . . . I'm so happy today to be again in those arms, to feel you to have you besides me, it seems as if every moment I lived for these 5 years was worth spending for this one moment. I missed you so much!!" Tanvi tightened her embrace.

"Now I know why you hated me so much . . . I cannot imagine what pain it caused you . . . but now I'm back . . . so everything is going to be fine . . ."

Tanvi nodded in agreement . . . they both again hugged each other . . . After a while Avani returned with Chirag, she went with him to buy ice-cream for him in the nearby ice-cream parlor.

Chirag stood their holding Avani's hand; he looked at his mom, who was comfortable in Madhav's arms, many questions reflecting in his innocent eyes. Madhav released Tanvi and started moving towards him, Chirag was not happy with what he saw, he was not used to of seeing his mom loving someone else other than him, He ran away and stood there alone, Tanvi went closer to him and said, "My shona is upset with me?"

Chirag didn't speak a word . . .

"What if I say your dad is back? You don't want to meet your dad? Won't you hug him and love him and return back all the love due all these years?"

On hearing that Chirag turned to her and rolled his eyes asking really? Tanvi nodded her head in agreement and promised she was telling truth . . .

"He won't leave me now?"

"Never, he will be with us forever now."

When Chirag came to know Madhav was his dad, his joy knew no bound, He went running to him and jumped to catch his shoulders. His anger vanished in seconds, he started chatting with him in his stammered voice, "You know Papa, at school everyone's dad use to come, I used to feel bad when at parents day, parents meetings only mom used to be there, where had you been? I remembered you every day and I prayed to god everyday to send you to me. See, he listened to me . . ."

Madhav hugged him tightly and kissed his cheeks.

"I know you prayed daily my dear, which is why I'm here today. Children's prayers never go unanswered, God sent me to meet you and he has promised me he will never let us separate . . ." Tanvi joined them and hugged both of them.

Chirag was smiling now. He was happy. He got down and ran to Sam Uncle's shop, He called everybody in the society to show his dad, everyone was happy to meet Madhav. They planned to have dinner at Chirang's favorite restaurant. Atharva also joined them for dinner; they both got very well mixed up. Madhav appreciated Avani's choice, he told her she was very lucky to have Atharva in her life and that he felt jealous of her that she had great love and friendship in her life . . . .

To this Atharva hugged him and said . . . "Not to worry dear . . . you too have a great love and he signaled towards Tanvi, for a friend . . . Main hoo na . . . . "and he copied Sharukh . . . Avani gave him a stop your filmy dialogs look and they both started fighting . . . after lot of efforts from Tanvi and Madhav they settled. Chirag was smiling at them. After everyone settled he commented, "They fight like small kids . . ." he said to Apeksha to which she agreed, that brought smile on everyone's face. After a long time Tanvi's heart was contented and happy. The reunion was celebrated in a splendid way to make it memorable. It was late night when they all returned back home. Madhav though was looking happy he had grown weak in these 5 days, he needed rest and Tanvi had noted that to herself, for the next week she had taken an off, Avani left with Chirag and she signaled her to take care of Maddy, wishing him faster recovery Atharva, Avani, Apeksha and Chirag left. Tanvi called the doctor and she did not let Madhav do anything. She sat beside him and cared for him like a baby, Madhav loved this feeling of belonging in her, They used to sit together and talk for hours, every sec with each other, he recovered quickly and was soon fit and back on track.

While Madhav was recovering friendship between Apeksha and Chirag bloomed in the days when Chirag stayed at Avani's place. They would be together for whole day, Apeksha was younger to Chirag by couple of years and so Chirag would dominate her, she would listen to him and agree to whatever he would say, he taught her to make the helicopter and frog out of paper which Madhav taught him, he would also boast about his drawing skills, he would not let any moment go waste. Soon they started bonding, Chirag would dominate her but also take care of her, he would not let her suffer, one day while playing the other kids in colony tease Apeksha while Chirag was not around, After he came to know about it from Apeksha he hit the kids with the Gulel from his pocket, they ran away, Apeksha took the gulel in her hand and said, "What is this?"

"This is called Gulel, My Dad has made this for me, when he was sitting there at the road side he taught me to pluck fruits with this by aiming at the fruits." Chirag proudly narrated it. He taught Apeksha to use Gulel though it was hard for her she just played around with it. Every day they would have a fight in between them and Avani and Atharva would have to come to rescue and make them talk to each other again, daily Apeksha would say im not going to talk to you, you are bad boy and then soon after a while they would be seen playing with each other. After Madhav recovered Tanvi and Madhav took him back to home, Chirag didnt want to go home, he was happy to be with Apeksha but when Madhav promised him to teach more new things he agreed to return to home. Next Sunday Madhav took Chirag to fishing and after trying for whole day at the end of day they could get hold of a small fish, Chirag was excited to see his first catch, Madhav took the fish home and Tanvi prepared delicious fish curry, the aura brought back the memories of the day they had sea food in Nisarg long back. While having the curry they decided to tell Tanvi's parents everything the next day, rather Madhav wanted to talk to them face to face, so next day they left for Ernakulum.

Tanvi's parents were more than happy to hear their daughter wanted to marry! Though Tanvi's parents wanted to have grand marriage she insisted to have it small, she wanted to avoid the media and public. They got married with simple rituals, with few family members and friends to grace the occasion. Chirag was so happy, he attended all rituals with great curiosity asking questions on everything that was being performed, observing every detail and grasping as much as he could. They stayed in Ernakulum for two weeks. Madhav and Tanvi decided to settle in TVM permanently, they bought a bungalow there. It was their first day at their new home in TVM. The stone Madhav had carved the song for Tanvi was placed on the adjacent wall to the main gate, serving as name plate with their names on top and song carved below . . . They both enter their new home to begin new life again.

"Kuch na kaho . . . Kuch bhi na kaho . . . kya kehna hai kya sunna hai . . . muzh ko pata hai . . . tum ko pata hai . . . samay ka ye paal tham sa gaya hai . . . Aur iss paal main . . . koi nahi hai . . . baas ek main hu baas ek tum ho!"

~.~.~.~.~.In the End there's a new Beginning. ~.~.~.~.